BLUEPRINT FOR A KISS

TAKE A CHANCE BOOK 3

NANCY WARREN

Blueprint for a Kiss, Take a Chance Book 3

Cover Design by Kim Killion

ISBN: ebook 978-1-928145-06-6

ISBN: print 978-1-928145-03-5

Ambleside Publishing

You can design a perfect life, then a woman comes along and messes it all up!

Prescott Chance is the go-to architect for the wealthy and famous, which has made him more wealthy and famous than he's ever wanted to be. He turns down more commissions than he accepts and is extremely private. Holly Legere is barely making ends meet between rent and student loans. As an assistant to Alistair Rupert, the notoriously difficult industrialist, she works night and day for slave wages, hanging on in hopes of a promised promotion in his huge organization. When Alistair Rupert's wife decides she wants a Prescott Chance designed house, and Prescott turns her down, it's Holly's job to make the choosy architect change his mind. And Holly is a very determined woman. In this modern romantic comedy, she'll go to any lengths to get him to design her boss a house, including pulling in his huge family for support.

∼

The best way to keep up with new releases and special offers is to join Nancy's newsletter at NancyWarrenAuthor.com

Holly Legere glanced at her cell phone to check the time and swore. She'd have claimed the damn thing was running fast except that even she had trouble arguing with satellites. San Francisco made her crazy anyway. She hated driving in this city and most of all she hated trying to park.

Already she was running a few minutes late for her meeting with the famous architect Prescott Chance which was adding to the stress that was her constant companion. It wasn't that she enjoyed being late, but her boss, the media mogul Alistair Rupert, always gave her more to do than any human could be expected to accomplish in a twenty-four hours day, and he threw fits when he didn't get everything he wanted, when he wanted and exactly how he wanted it. Alistair had told her to see the architect and get him to design Alistair and his scary wife a house after the architect had refused the commission.

She wasn't thrilled with her current assignment. How was she supposed to get Prescott Chance, one of the most famous and most in-demand architects in the world, to change his mind and build a house for her boss?

Secretly, she was happy someone had said no to Rupert. But her boss had not become a bazillionaire by taking no for an answer. He also hadn't become a bazillionaire by treating employees well, respecting union agreements or showing any regard at all for the environment. But, she reminded herself as she came off the Golden Gate and slowed infinitesimally for some poor tourist who didn't know you couldn't stop at the toll booths, beggars can't be choosers.

Her degrees in communications followed by an MBA left her well suited to work in media or publishing, two declining industries that were shedding a lot more people than they were hiring.

She'd ended up as a gofer for the wealthy industrialist and was happy to have any kind of a job that let her pay her student loans and the rent. She could even eat if she gave up such extravagances as cheese and wine.

Sometimes she thought heaven was one big wine and cheese party.

She found the offices of PGC Architects and drove around the block. Of course there was no parking. The minutes ticked past as she tried a leafy side street and ended up having to back out again as a big semi was laying right across the road like a fallen tree. Seriously flustered now— she drove round the block again and—thank the good Lord, a car pulled out of the tiny lane beside the PGC office. She stopped so fast that her briefcase flew off the passenger seat and onto the floor, spilling paper everywhere. *Crap.* She wedged her car into the tiny spot, shoved the paper back into the briefcase and took a much-needed moment to breathe. A quick glance in the rearview showed that her corkscrew curls were beyond help. A swipe of lip gloss was the best she could do for her appearance. And, she reminded herself, a positive attitude.

She got out of the car, locked it behind her and headed into PGC, refusing to rush. She was the client, she reminded herself.

Walking into PGC was an amazing experience. She hadn't even noticed the noise and bustle of the streets outside, not until the door closed softly behind her and she was struck by the silence. She felt as though she were entering a church.

She walked up to a sleek reception desk, black and curved, where an equally sleek young woman in a blond chignon and chunky black glasses regarded her with raised brows.

"Hi," she said. Then lowered her voice. "Holly Legere. I'm here to see Prescott Chance."

She could not imagine a working office could be so quiet. Then, she looked around and saw a stairway rising up and on the other side of the stairway a large office area behind glass. Inside, there was the bustle she'd expected to find, rows of desks, people hunched over computers, talking in groups, someone working on the model of what looked to be an apartment building. Maybe an office tower. She bet if she walked through the double doors she'd enter a fairly noisy environment. But out here? It was as silent as a cathedral.

The woman flicked a glance at a screen. "I'm so sorry. You've missed your appointment."

People did not blow off her boss like that. And she couldn't let them do it to her. This gig was important. Vital to her budding career. "I didn't miss it. I'm a little late. Traffic was murder."

"I understand, really I do. Mr. Chance left a message for

you." And she handed over a handwritten note. Holly blinked. She could not remember the last time she'd received a note with, like, ink on paper. It was as quaint as getting a letter in the mail.

The note said, "I never change my mind."

Holly read the note a second time and glanced up to the receptionist. "Who does he think he is? God?"

"I like to think of him more as a superhero. Mysterious, but powerful."

She leaned closer, sensing an ally. "I could get fired over this."

The woman looked sympathetic but unhelpful. "I'm really sorry," she said. The words, *next time be on time* floated out there, louder for remaining unspoken.

Holly left the hallowed space and hit the street feeling hot, irritable and mad at herself. It was a beautiful September day, sunny and fogless, but that didn't lift her mood. Why hadn't she allowed more time to get here? But she always tried to shoehorn too many things into too few hours, and sometimes the hours didn't stretch the way she wished they would. If she had a superpower, that's what hers would be. She'd balloon hours when she needed more time and also shrink them when she was stuck with extra time so she could bank the extra minutes.

She got into her car and immediately pulled out her cell. Alistair Rupert wasn't going to be happy.

"He agreed, yes?" were Rupert's first crisp words.

"Actually, no. He said no."

There was a silence and she pulled the phone away from her ear in case he started shouting at her. Instead, he said, "Holly, I hired you because you are a resourceful girl." *Girl? Really?* "I trust you can get him to change his mind."

"He said he never changes his mind." And she had that in writing.

"Let me put it to you simply. My wife wants a Prescott Chance home. The happiness of my marriage is hanging on this. Your job depends on getting Prescott Chance to agree to design my house. Do not come back until he's agreed."

"And if he doesn't?"

"Then don't come back at all."

She wanted to tell him where he could stick his job, but the weight of her student loans got in the way. One day, she swore to herself, she'd be independently wealthy so she could tell people like Rupert to shove it.

The click in her ear told her the conversation was over.

A hopeful motorist saw her sitting in her car and slowed but she waved them on.

Pros and cons. She thought Rupert was a twit. But he was a powerful one and she'd taken the job as a personal assistant hoping to prove herself enough to get a real job in his empire. His businesses were huge and she knew there were plum jobs with her name on them if she could get him to promote her before he fired her. She blew out a breath that made a curl dance on her forehead. Rupert was the kind of man who was your best friend one day and shoving a knife in your ribs the next. But it was a job. And she needed that job.

And he was right. She was resourceful.

She got out of her car and did some sleuthing. There were three cars parked right behind PGC. She had to assume that one of the spots was reserved for the great Prescott Chance himself.

The car in the center was a Tesla. Well, that was easy. Everything she knew about Prescott Chance, that he was rich, forward-thinking, green and loved elegant design pointed to him being the owner of that sleek, black car.

Now all she had to do was the one thing she was worst at.

She had to wait.

She pulled out her tablet computer and called up her research file on Prescott Chance. There must be something she could do to get him to change his mind.

She pulled up a profile article on the architect and enlarged the photo. In it, Prescott Chance sat cross-legged, his hands resting on the earth. He might be posing for a photo but it looked as though he'd forgotten the photographer was even there. He had the look of a Zen master or a mystic, albeit a gorgeous one. He had black hair, a long, elegant face and eyes that seemed to gaze into a different world. He apparently sat for hours before he ever began designing. Unlike her, he was never in a rush. The article quoted him saying, "I believe an architect needs to take time to absorb the organic wholeness of a site. I have to walk the area, breathe the air, watch the light as the sun rises and as it changes throughout the day. I need to understand the indigenous trees and shrubs, the weather patterns. I need to know and respect the earth."

Poser.

"Until I understand a site the way a man might try to understand the many moods of a beloved woman, I don't even touch a pencil or paper."

Oh, as if.

Even as she scoffed, she had to admit to loving the man's work. His buildings, whether public or private, were unique. Not dramatic or showy, but they fit with their surroundings.

According to the journalist, Prescott Chance did not own a cell phone because he never, ever wanted to be distracted when he was working. He owned no device that beeped or squeaked or rang. If someone at the office needed him badly enough they could track him down. And if he was working in the office with his door closed, one of his associates said, "God help the fool who knocked on that door."

He refused more commissions than he accepted, never promised a specific completion date, and was famous for refusing to cater to his clients' whims.

"It's like hiring Rain Man to design your house," an A List celebrity had once complained.

Instead of leaving him broke, his whims and crotchets had helped make him famous and very rich. He was one of the most sought after architects in the world because he might be difficult but he was also a brilliant visionary. His final quote in the article was, "If one of my designs calls attention to itself then I have failed. A good design blends into its surroundings and exists in harmony with the land."

And if he turned down a project nothing would entice him to change his mind. Throw money at him, he yawned. One enterprising earl, desperate to get Prescott to rebuild a crumbling castle, had even promised to wrangle him a knighthood. Prescott had been supremely uninterested in the title. "The castle doesn't speak to me," he said.

"What does speak to you?" the journalist had asked, and Holly could have kissed the man for asking the question she so needed answered.

She read the next part of the article eagerly: "Chance pauses, taking his time to think and finally, he says, 'Challenge.'"

"What kind of challenge?"

"Chance has a way of considering a question as though it's a Zen koan. Finally, he answers, 'I know it when I see it.'"

And wasn't that helpful. Well, she wasn't a quitter and

that *I never change my mind* note had her doubly determined. He was messing with the wrong girl. He wanted a
challenge?

Oh, she was going to give Prescott Chance a challenge,
all right.

CHAPTER 2

*P*rescott Chance stepped out of his office with one thing on his mind. He wanted to get to Petaluma in time for the sunset. An idea was forming around a project but he needed to gauge the light and simply sit for a bit.

He had nothing with him but his car fob and his wallet. He said goodbye to his staff and headed out the back door to his car. He was almost beside it when he realized there was a woman sitting on the hood.

A mass of untidy curls sparked red gold in the sunlight. She had big green eyes and a sprinkle of freckles, a generous mouth and a very determined looking chin.

For a moment neither said anything. He didn't see the point in stating the obvious. She was sitting on his car. She didn't look like a homeless person or a particularly crazy one. He assumed she'd tell him her reason. A visual man, Prescott never forgot a face and he knew he'd never seen this one before.

She suddenly broke into a grin that seemed more natural to her than the stern look he'd first encountered.

She hopped off his car and extended her hand. "Mr. Chance. I'm Holly Legere. We missed our meeting today and it's really important that I speak with you. I'm Alistair Rupert's assistant. I'd really like a few minutes of your time."

Ah, yes. Alistair Rupert was not the first big shot to think he could have a Prescott Chance design because he wanted one and could afford it, but he was wrong. Sending an unpunctual and untidy intern to beg his cause wasn't going to help. "I won't change my mind."

"I'm not asking you to. He understands that the property you looked at didn't work for you." She took a breath. "The thing is, Mr. Rupert wants you to find a piece of property that speaks to you. He's going to let you choose it."

"He'd be better to find another architect." He moved toward the driver's side which involved going around Holly Legere. But as he tried to skirt around, she stepped in front of him. Her white shirt had come untucked from her skirt and he fought the urge to tell her to tuck it back in.

"Please. I am not one to beg and believe me I wish I didn't have to, but my job is on the line here."

He could see that she was telling the truth. The woman looked as though she weren't getting enough sleep. Her big green eyes glowed with sincerity and faint lines of strain showed on her face.

"I'd like to help you." Even though that was a platitude, it was true. He didn't want to see a young woman lose her job in a tough economy, and he didn't want to be involved in a stranger's job loss even peripherally. "But I can't wander around looking for building sites." He decided to tell her the full truth. "Also, I didn't like your boss."

She laughed and then slapped her hand over her mouth as though the mirth had slipped out by accident. "I don't like him either but he's absolutely determined."

Prescott didn't like arguing so he simply stood there quietly hoping she'd go away.

She didn't. After studying him for a few moments she said, "I tell you what. I will find five sites that I think you might like. If one of them speaks to you, you'll build on it. If none of them does I'll accept defeat."

"And why would I waste my time going to five building sites for a man I don't like?"

She leaned closer and he caught a scent of something that reminded him of wildflowers. "Because I'm going to find a site that is so perfect you will be inspired to do your greatest work."

He lifted a brow. Was that the best she could do? "You have no idea what inspires me."

"I've read everything I could find about you." She pulled her shoulders up, looking like someone making a resolution. "I can find your perfect site."

He looked at her, those eyes brimming with sincerity and determination. "You forgot to offer me a large sum of money."

She saw through his bluff immediately. "Please. Money doesn't motivate you."

"Are you sure you know what motivates me?" He hadn't meant the words as a sexual dare, but when he saw her eyes widen and a slight blush suddenly stain her cheeks he felt an instant awareness crackle between them.

Damn. He didn't have time for this. And this untidy woman whose cell phone was even now buzzing somewhere about her was not his type. He was just shaken enough by the unwanted attraction that he did a very uncharacteristic thing. He said, "Okay. You got your meeting. Find me a site you think will speak to me and we'll see."

"Five sites," she argued, making him immediately regret

his impulse to help her out. "You will look at five sites and if one of them speaks to you you'll design Rupert's house."

In spite of himself he was amused. He'd managed to streamline his life to the point that no one ever argued with him these days. It was almost a novelty to have this woman pushing at him without a staff member shielding him from distraction. "Usually, when a person is bargaining, they have something to offer." Even as the words left his mouth he saw how they could be misconstrued, so he rapidly added, "Why are you doing all this for a man who will never appreciate one of my designs?"

She met his gaze with her own frank look. "Desperation."

As Holly drove back to the dumpy apartment she shared in The Mission, the traditionally Latino section of San Francisco, she tried to congratulate herself that she'd won the battle and would keep her job. At least for now.

To celebrate, she called her roommate Luis and they agreed to go out to one of their favorite taco places. Luis's family was from The Mission and he knew all the best and cheapest places to eat.

As they sat over a plate of tacos and a beer in a tiny, family-run place on Mission Street, she told him about her meeting.

She'd met Luis when she'd searched for affordable places to live in the Bay area. The rents were horrendous, the vacancy rate almost negative and so she'd widened her field from a studio to sharing. She'd been hesitant about living with a guy but five minutes in Luis's company had convinced her. He was funny, hip, loved to cook and his bookshelves were as crowded as hers, though his books were in both Spanish and English.

He'd told her right away that he had a girlfriend, Maria, who was a hairdresser. "Why isn't she sharing the apartment with you?" she'd asked him.

He shook his head sadly. "Traditional family."

So, Maria lived with her family a few streets away and they turned a blind eye to the number of nights she didn't come home. Since Holly liked Maria—who could also cook—the arrangement suited all of them. One day, she knew, those two would get married and she'd have to find another place, but by then she hoped to be on her feet financially.

Besides, Rupert kept her so busy she was barely ever home, and when she was she was squeezed into the desk in her room calculating time zones. She'd started using an Internet app to schedule messages to his many international clients so she could at least snatch a few hours of sleep a night.

The carrot Rupert dangled in front her was that anyone who managed to stay with him for a year or two as his assistant got promoted within his empire. However, when she asked around, it turned out that he'd fired three former assistants, two assistants had quit, one suffered a nervous breakdown and only two had survived to get that promised promotion.

Even though the odds were against her, Holly knew she had the guts and determination to get through a year or two of hell to get her feet firmly on the ladder of corporate success.

She'd worked hard in business school, often chronically short of sleep between her college workload and the various jobs she's held down in order to make ends meet. She was used to the life.

Short term pain, she told herself several times a day.

It seemed that no sooner did she get a handle on one part of Rupert's crazy demands than he ramped up another area. This was the first time he'd threatened to fire her and she'd been with him seven months. According to Christophe, the German/American who was one of the two assistants to go on to one of those plum jobs, she was doing exceedingly well. "By the time I'd been there seven months Rupert had threatened to fire me at least four times."

She wasn't sure she could cope with that kind of pressure. She'd never been fired from anything in her life. And one self-involved architect was not going to be her stumbling block.

"So you told this guy you're going to find him five building sites," Luis commented when she'd finished telling him her slightly unorthodox plan.

"I did, didn't I?" She'd been so caught up in making sure Prescott Chance agreed to work with her that she'd come up with the crazy plan on the spur of the moment, then kept pushing until the architect agreed.

"Chica, how are you going to find building sites that a famous architect doesn't know about?"

It was a reasonable question. Unfortunately, she had no answer. She stuck a taco chip in salsa. "He was going to drive away. I had to stop him and that was all I could think of. I'll figure something out. I'll have to."

"He's like the Frank Gehry of the new millennium," Luis said, echoing a headline in *Architectural Digest* that had in fact used almost those exact words. "What's he like in person?" Luis asked, reaching for another taco.

She tried to articulate her first impressions of Prescott Chance. "Still." It was the first word that came to mind.

"Still like immobile?"

"Like still waters run deep." She thought back to when she'd first seen him; how she'd been struck by the thoughtful expression on his face and how, when they'd talked, he'd never fidgeted or talked too much. He moved when necessary, spoke when necessary. "It's almost like he's a vampire or something living in society and trying to blend in but you look at him and somehow know he's different."

"He's scary?"

"No. More self-contained I guess. I mean, I read up on him, everything I could find, and he's famous for being disconnected. He doesn't do social media, he has no cell phone."

Luis snorted. "Come on. Everybody has a cell phone." He gestured to the three phones even now sitting on the table between them. "You can't do business without one."

She shook her head. "In the few interviews he's ever given he says he connects with the landscape and with his vision. He doesn't want to be distracted."

Luis looked disbelieving. "He's posing."

"I thought so too until I met him. Now I'm not so sure."

"He lives in San Francisco and doesn't do social media?" Luis was always complaining about how the city was being ruined by all the programmers who'd taken over the town since Facebook and Google were headquartered there. "It's like moving to Napa and being a teetotaler."

"I know. You have to admire it a little bit."

Since both she and Luis were pretty much married to their smartphones, she felt a pang of envy that anyone could be freed from their phone. Two of those phones on the table were hers. One was basically Alistair Rupert's 24/7 hotline to her.

She and Luis had a deal when they were out together that he could only pick up for Maria and she could only pick up for Rupert. Which gave them approximately half of their time together without one or both on the phone or texting. She sipped her beer absently. Then grinned. "Do you remember when I took up meditating?"

"How could I ever forget those four minutes?"

"Exactly. I was so twitchy and fidgety and my mind was racing. I can't stay still for one minute. But Prescott Chance is the kind of man who could be a Zen master. I bet he could sit in silence and stillness for a week and not even notice."

"You're right. That is scary."

"Not as scary as me out of a job. So, think, how do I come up with building sites that will inspire a famously eccentric architect?"

Luis was one of those software designers he claimed were ruining the city. He refused to work for the big companies though. He was involved in a startup that would be lucrative if it ever got off the ground. Right now he was barely scraping by but still, he knew this city. His family had lived here for generations. Luis was connected. "Money's no object?"

"Please. We're talking Alistair Rupert. His wife wants a Chance-designed home. He's the Prada of architects and she wants hers. Naturally, Chance despises most of the people who want his services, which has only made him more desirable." She grinned suddenly. "Can you imagine being rich enough to have anything you want? And then having an architect say no to you? That's got to hurt."

"It's a problem I wouldn't mind having," Luis said glumly, eyeing the last taco.

She waved her hand at him, telling him to go ahead and eat it. "I wouldn't mind either," she admitted. "And Iona, Rupert's wife, is even more scary than Rupert. I mean, she did not marry the man for his looks or charm. He's thirty years older than her, chubby and mean. So imagine putting up with Alistair Rupert to get access to all that money and then have some guy throw it back."

"I think it's cool."

She nodded. "As much as I need him to change his mind, I admire him saying no to Rupert. Nobody says no to Rupert."

"Does he want waterfront? Acreage in Sonoma? Right in the city? What does Rupert want?"

"Honestly, I don't think Rupert cares. He's got offices in five cities and minions like me doing all his leg work. If Mrs. Rupert is happy, then he's happy. A Prescott Chance house would be a lot cheaper than a third high-profile divorce. And Mrs. Rupert wants a Prescott Chance house."

"Too bad Mrs. Rupert doesn't want to live in The Mission. My grandparents are selling," he said, looking glum.

"Oh, no." She'd met his grandparents. They'd lived in the Hispanic district for fifty years.

"All their friends are moving out and none of the kids can afford to move back here." He scowled. "If my startup had taken off by now I might try to buy it, but I can't afford to live here either. Trouble is, the house is kind of run down and the lot is a weird shape. Like a trapezoid. You need an architect with wacky ideas to get any hope of a good price, and they need the money to retire on."

She shook her head sadly. "I really can't see Mrs. Rupert —or Mr. Rupert—in The Mission."

WHEN HOLLY WALKED into PGC Architects the next Monday afternoon, having killed a half hour at a coffee shop because she was so early for her appointment, the sleek young woman, wearing gray this time, did a double take when she saw her.

"Hi," she said, friendly because she was always friendly. "I'm here to see Prescott."

The woman looked as though she might be contemplating pushing a secret button that would summon security, so Holly quickly said, "He's expecting me."

"Prescott Chance is expecting you?" She did a quick glance at her computer screen where no doubt his schedule was laid out. Mostly blank she imagined.

"Yes. We're seeing a building lot today."

As though she couldn't stop herself, the woman leaned forward and said, "I have never known him to change his mind."

Holly figured one confidence deserved another so she, in her turn, leaned in. "You have never known me when I am terrified to lose my job, which would mean getting kicked out of my rental and defaulting on my student loans."

She nodded as though she might know all about tight budgets, being young and in the city and all. "I've worked here for three years and I have never seen him change his mind. That's impressive."

She felt her confidence bounce. "Thanks."

In the week since Prescott had tried to blow her off she'd spent every spare second she had researching possible sites for Chez Rupert. Not that there were many seconds when she wasn't running around after Rupert doing everything from coordinating international meetings and interviewing ghost writers for a business book he planned to write, to picking up his dry cleaning if his driver was too busy ferrying Mrs. Rupert. What little ego she'd had as a freshly minted MBA was pretty much squeezed out of her.

She had top real estate agents in four countries on speed dial. Rupert and his wife were willing to consider the United States (either coast, but nothing in the middle), Switzerland, certain parts of the UK where Rupert was originally from, or one of several islands in the Caribbean. However, she'd already nixed the latter, knowing Rupert would never live on an island in the middle of nowhere. He liked the energy of big cities. If he wasn't in one he'd need to be near it. Dealing with the competing wishes of Mr. and Mrs. Rupert made her wish she'd received a psychology degree instead of business ones.

Also, there was the problem of getting Prescott Chance to look at a site that involved a plane journey. He didn't want to design the Ruperts a house at all. She couldn't imagine him flying far to look at a prospective property. However, she was keeping her options open and really hoping something cropped up that was within a day's driving radius.

This was California, for heaven's sake. The real estate agents had tried to show her every high-end listing in their portfolios, most of them whisper listings, so called because you wouldn't find them publicly listed. No sign ever sat out on the front lawn. Only super-qualified buyers even heard about them.

Even at the highest of the high end she'd had to be brutally selective. She'd already toured three prospective properties and knew they wouldn't work. But the fourth one, she'd liked. It was in Pacific Heights, an older estate with a view of the Golden Gate. The agent called it the jewel in the crown of his exclusive portfolio and she could see why. The building didn't matter; it was the land that was spectacular. An acre of gorgeous with views to die for. She could imagine what Prescott could achieve. Based on his portfolio, which she knew almost as intimately as he did, she pictured him sitting cross-legged on the lawn, inspired by the beauty of the spot with the few natural challenges of a creek and a gorgeous cluster of redwoods that couldn't be cut down.

She knew that while Rupert was cheap with his staff and a notorious skinflint in his business dealings, he was extremely generous when spending money on himself and his Russian wife, so Holly didn't even blink at the price or the additional cost of knocking down the existing mansion to build a new one.

While she was mentally crossing her fingers that she'd found the right site, Prescott Chance walked down the stairs, from what must be his office high above the noisy workers. He strode to where she was standing. It was completely spooky. She hadn't seen the chic receptionist call or text and yet he'd appeared.

Luis was always regaling her with stories of communication technologies being invented or experimented with. Some of them involved thought communication, which scared more than impressed her.

Anyone trying to get through on her thought frequency would likely get a busy signal.

He didn't have so much as a pencil in his hand. She had never known anyone to travel so light.

"I'll see you tomorrow," was all he said to the blond.

"Okay."

And they walked out into the noise and breeze of a city she'd temporarily forgotten existed. "Was that some kind of mind communication you used in there?" she asked.

"Pardon?"

"I never saw the receptionist alert you in any way that I was there and then you appeared like magic."

He looked at her like she might be a few face cards short of a full deck. "I saw you arrive through the window in my office."

So much for high tech. "Oh." Then she reminded herself that he'd changed his mind because of her, something he reportedly hadn't done in at least three years, so she grabbed back her feeling of confidence, knowing she'd need it to deal with Prescott Chance. "Would you like me to drive?" She really hoped he'd say no because although she'd remembered to fill up with gas, and she'd even plugged in a couple of dollars to the vacuum at the gas station, nothing was ever going to make her twelve-year-old car look newer. Or nicer.

He glanced at her in surprise. "Are we traveling together?" He didn't seem like he was insulted by the notion, more surprised.

"Well, I guess we could meet there, but I was going to give you the background on the property on the way."

"I'll drive," he said, and clicked the fancy fob that opened the doors and started the engine or battery or whatever made this thing run.

The real estate agent was already there when they arrived at the property. A friendly guy in his forties, he held a personalized folder and strode toward Prescott with a broad smile on his face and his free hand outstretched. "Well, Prescott Chance, it is a real honor to meet you. I'm Frank Norbert."

Prescott shook his hand briefly and waved away the folder, which the agent then handed to her. Normally, of course, he'd be selling to the end buyer, but Holly had already explained that Prescott was the one who would determine what the Ruperts purchased. It might be unorthodox but she figured for the size of commission that must be involved here, Frank Norbert would put up with a little unorthodox. He hastened after Prescott, who had already walked through the open gate.

She followed behind, watching Prescott, hoping he loved the property as much as she had. Please let him make one part of her job a tiny bit easier.

No possible way to tell what he was thinking from his expression. Frank Norbert was extolling the various features of the property, most of which were evident. The morning fog had burned off and the sun was shining for which she was grateful. As she walked behind the two men, she heard Frank point out the green lawn that glowed with health, a water feature that babbled, the old stone walls, the trees, the mature landscaping, the view. Frank didn't bother even mentioning the house. Instead he focused on height restrictions, building envelopes and something about a soil drainage test. He was in the middle of telling Prescott about the neighborhood when the architect interrupted him.

"Holly?"

"Yes?"

He'd never used her name before. She wasn't certain he knew it so it was startling to hear him call her Holly. "Could I see you for a moment?"

"Yes, sure." She sent a quick smile to Frank and followed Prescott as he strode to the edge of the stone patio. She looked at him with her eyebrows raised. He looked as calm as ever, but he cut his eyes to where Frank stood a few feet away checking his cell phone.

"Make him stop talking."

"Make him stop talking?" He was an agent trying to sell a property.

"I need to feel a site and let it communicate with me, and I cannot do it with a salesman babbling in my ear."

"I completely understand," she said, reminding herself that she was in the presence of an artist famous for being temperamental.

She walked back to where Frank stood. Smiled. "He needs a few moments alone to feel the earth."

He nodded, looking impressed. "Right, I read he's descended from a line of Cherokee warriors and that he's some kind of shaman."

She'd read that too. But having worked seven months for Alistair Rupert, she knew all about how famous men manipulated their images. "Maybe we could sit out front and discuss price and timing and so on. Mrs. Rupert's very anxious to get started, so as soon as Prescott approves a property they'll want to move fast."

"Of course, anything I can do to help. Anything at all. It would be my pleasure."

She walked him around to the front of the house, hopefully out of earshot so Prescott could commune with the earth spirits of Pacific Heights or talk to its aura or whatever he needed to do.

She just hoped that they gave him the thumbs-up.

Within ten minutes, Prescott returned. She glanced up, a question in her eyes, but he'd been there such a short time that her stomach was already dropping when he shook his head. "No."

"No?" Frank strode forward ready to launch into a sales pitch, overcome objections, whatever you did to turn around a sale, but Prescott simply got in his car and shut the door, leaving the bewildered agent standing there looking foolish.

"Well," Frank said, looking at her as though she might have some clue as to why Prescott Chance behaved so oddly but she didn't. All she knew was that she wasn't hanging around here explaining Prescott's brusque behavior, or he might leave without her.

"I'll be in touch," she said, shaking hands briefly and then dashing to the passenger side of the Tesla.

She'd barely settled when the car reversed.

"Well," she said, "what did that poor man ever do to you?"

"Nothing." He seemed surprised she would ask.

"But you were so rude to him."

"No, I wasn't. I dislike small talk. I didn't ask him to come, and I don't have time to waste telling him why I'm not going to design a house on that lot."

"Why won't you?" she almost wailed. "I thought that spot would be perfect. You could imagine looking up and seeing a Prescott Chance on the crown of that fantastic property. It would be a real showplace."

"If you look at a building and think about the architect, then the architect has failed," he said simply.

"But how do you know? When it's right? Come on, throw me a bone here. I've got four chances left. Why waste everybody's time? Wouldn't it be easier for all of us if you gave me a few clues so I could find the right spot sooner rather than later?"

He seemed to give the matter deep thought. Then he said, "When I find the right place for me to design, it's like the structure's already there. It was always there waiting to be uncovered. And when I'm finished and I've got the design absolutely right and the builders don't screw it up, then, at the end you look at that building and realize it was inevitable."

"Well," she said brightly. "That should help."

"Architecture should speak of its time and place but yearn for timelessness," he added.

"Frank Gehry said that. I saw it quoted on your firm's website."

"That's what I believe. It's an organic thing, that the design should be part of the landscape and not draw attention to itself."

"Kind of like good fashion sense," she said.

He turned to look at her in surprise and she felt like explaining that she understood good fashion sense, she simply didn't have it.

Unlike him. He seemed always to look as sleek as a panther, in dark neutrals, black and gray and navy, but the cut of every piece of his clothing was exquisite. She suspected he had all his clothes hand made by designers in Italy.

Challenge, she reminded herself. He'd admitted he thrived on challenge.

So, it seemed, did she. And now she had to find another perfect site while Rupert grew increasingly testy and her job grew increasingly tenuous.

CHAPTER 3

The second place she showed Prescott was a gated estate overlooking the ocean in Marin County.

The neighbor to one side was an aging movie star, which would make Iona Rupert happy. The next closest neighbor was a bank president. If there were ever a neighborhood barbecue, Rupert would have somebody to talk to.

The property had belonged to a quirky artist in the thirties then been renovated by more recent owners who, to Holly's eyes, didn't have much taste. The mansion wasn't officially listed when she received the call. Working for the super rich really did have advantages.

She thought Prescott would like the site which was stepped so he could design something layered if he wanted to.

With the ocean at its foot and a secluded garden at its head she thought the place begged for a genius architect. And since the star of the show here was always going to be the ocean and the sunsets, she felt confident he'd never feel like his design was competing with nature. No architect was that good.

This time, she warned the agent in advance what Prescott was like and tactfully suggested she give him the space and quiet he needed to commune with the plot of land. This agent was a stunning woman in her thirties who exuded confidence and wore accessories in a way that Holly could never get right. On her, that scarf would blow away, and if she tried to wear a gold bracelet it would probably catch on things.

Forewarned and forearmed, the agent stayed in the background, but Holly could see she was checking Prescott out. He was so gorgeous you couldn't help it. He caught her looking at him and Holly got the sense that he was used to female interest.

She'd have to remember that. She wasn't the only woman who found him disturbingly attractive if you liked the remote, difficult type.

This time he stayed twenty minutes but, just when she began to feel hopeful, she got the heart-sinking shake of the head.

Damn. However, she noticed that with the hot female real estate agent, he took her card, let her shake his hand a little longer than business protocol dictated.

"I'm sorry, Holly," he said, and she felt like he meant it. Probably he was reacting to the dark circles under her eyes from lack of sleep.

Okay, she'd struck out twice with ocean views. The third property was hidden away in the hills. No house had ever been built on it, which she thought might help him envision his own creation among the towering trees and the rocky slopes. There were acres and acres of land. He wanted a challenge? This unique property would be a blank canvas.

He spent so long walking the property, stopping every now and then to inspect the ground or to sit on a rock and stare out at the mountains around him that she began to feel hopeful.

"I'm sorry, Holly," he said, again sounding like he actually was when he turned her down the third time. "I want to help you, but I can't feel it."

"Couldn't you fake it? Couldn't you, for once, maybe see what it feels like to create something that isn't from a vision? That you actually have to work at designing?" She was so frustrated she knew she was being rude, but she couldn't seem to stop herself. Maybe he'd only looked at three properties but she'd looked at dozens in person, scanned thousands online.

Rupert, who used to snarl at her when he came into the office in the morning, now ignored her, which she sensed was worse.

"I don't work that way." And there it was. The simple egotism of the genius.

Over a homemade batch of margaritas and a pizza later that night she wailed to Luis and Maria about her problems.

"The economy's picking up, you know, you should start looking for another job," Luis said. "Get hold of some head-hunters." Which was Luis speak for look out, chica, your ass is grass.

Maria let them talk and nibbled pizza, her big brown eyes following the conversation even though she said little.

Finally, when there was a pause because both Luis and Holly had shoved too much pizza in their mouths at the same moment, she said. "You should see where he grew up."

Holly turned to stare at Maria. Still chewing, she motioned her to go on.

Maria shrugged as though they were missing something completely obvious to her. "Family. That's a person's biggest influence. You said he grew up in Oregon. Maybe try to find something that would appeal to that part of him. The big trees and the rain."

Holly was nodding, feeling like smacking herself in the head for being so dense. She wiped her hands rapidly on the paper towel they were using instead of napkins and then grabbed her laptop. She had Prescott Chance's entire portfolio on her computer as well as every bit of background information she'd been able to unearth. She scanned through them for about the millionth time then nodded. "He grew up in a place called Hidden Falls, Oregon. I wonder if any of his family still lives there. Parents maybe."

Luis said, "Why? Are you planning on dropping in on his mom for tea?"

She nodded, realizing that Prescott might quote even more famous architects than himself when she asked him specifically what he liked, but his mother, if she knew mothers, would have concrete answers. "That is exactly what I'm going to do. Who knows a person better than their mother?"

"Are you crazy?" Luis asked.

"No," Maria said. "It's a good plan."

At least, she was desperate enough that she hoped so.

Holly was one who no sooner made a decision than she was on the move. While she sipped the last half of her margarita, she texted Rupert's personal secretary to tell her that she was looking at properties farther up the coast tomorrow so she wouldn't be in the office. With her phones and laptop she pretty much had a mobile setup anyway.

With Bluetooth she could make calls as she drove, which she explained to Luis as she dug under the couch cushions in search of her missing sunglasses.

"Why don't you fly? You'd be there in no time."

"Because I am going to look at properties on my way up the coast." The nice thing about shopping for the very highest of the top end of the market was that real estate agents were always available.

Within two hours of her decision she had confirmed that Prescott's parents still lived in the same house where he'd grown up. And she had several properties lined up to see.

She focused on land that had never been built on and specified that there could be no historical native burial sites. Prescott was very vocal about respecting native traditional lands.

Because it was a Friday, she could take her time driving back, look at some more land.

DAPHNE CHANCE OPENED the door and blinked in surprise at the young woman standing there. She was a stranger with red-blonde hair that insisted on curling into messy ringlets exactly like Daphne's own.

"Daphne Chance?" the young woman said.

"Yes?"

"My name is Holly Legere. I am so sorry to bother you but I am wondering if I could talk to you about your son, Prescott."

Her mother's instinct was one of alarm. "Is he all right?"

"Yes," the young woman hastily assured her. "I didn't put that right." She took a quick breath and blew it out. "I'm tired and stressed and kind of nervous. I was hoping you could give me some information about your son. It's kind of a last-ditch attempt. I'm sorry to burst in on you like this. I tried to call, but there was no answer. You don't seem to have any kind of answering service."

Daphne stifled a smile. She couldn't count the times that

some lovestruck young girl had phoned her or snuck by for a visit when Prescott was out to ask for advice. But it had been years since she'd had such a visit. As she'd done when the kids were in high school, she opened the door wide and said, "Come in. We had an answering machine but it broke. My husband is trying to fix it. In the meantime, we do without."

The girl heaved a sigh of relief. Had she really thought she'd turn her away? She'd do what she'd always done. Listen to this nice young woman and then gently suggest that Daphne couldn't make her son fall in love with her any more than she'd been able to make him fall for any of the others through the years. Some days she wondered if he'd ever get out of his own head long enough to fall in love with any woman.

However it quickly became apparent that it wasn't love driving this woman but economics. "I need to find a building site that speaks to Prescott Chance or I will lose my job."

"Good heavens. How drastic." She didn't know what else to say.

The woman stood fidgeting in her hallway. "My boss is Alistair Rupert."

"Oh." That pretty much explained everything. Alistair Rupert was hated by unions since he relished busting them, he was hated by environmentalists, by most politicians and by a string of girlfriends and ex-wives. Journalists loved him because between the business scandals and messy divorces he was always making news. He was an East Londoner and proud of it, and his colorful expressions were usually good for a sound bite.

She couldn't imagine working for the man. "I'm not sure how I can help, but would you like some tea?"

"I really would. I drove all the way from San Francisco hoping you could help me."

"I'll get some cookies to go with that tea," she said, earning her an impish grin.

As Daphne led the way into the kitchen to put on tea, Holly said, "This is where Prescott grew up?"

"Yep. Pretty humble origins, huh?"

"No. That wasn't what I meant. It's just so—" She glanced around the place and Daphne was able to finish her sentence for her.

"Chaotic. I know. I've got eleven kids and a husband and a dog. I've lived with chaos and clutter so long I think I'd go crazy if I suddenly had order and peace and quiet. But Scott always kept his space clutter free. He never liked distractions."

Holly nodded. "Scott? That's what you call him?"

"Yes. But ever since he left home he's used his full name: Prescott."

"Mrs. Chance, I need to understand what inspires him." As Daphne watched that expressive face, the hands that were never still, the hair that bounced and swayed as she talked, the vivid eyes, the energy radiating, she thought, no. It's not simple economics driving her. It was about passion.

There was something about Holly that drew Daphne's interest and sympathy. The young woman had dark circles under her eyes and a slightly harried look to her. She looked as though she needed a few good nights' sleep and a day at the spa. "Please, call me Daphne."

When she put the kettle on and settled her unexpected guest at the big kitchen table, she pushed the mass of salad greens aside.

"I've interrupted you, I'm so sorry."

"No. It's fine." Then, with the motherly pride she

couldn't help, she said, "One of my sons is getting married. It's our first wedding in the family."

"That's wonderful." Instead of sitting at the table, her unexpected guest grabbed a carrot peeler and began scraping the carrots that were piled near three massive heads of assorted lettuces. "Did you say eleven children?"

"Yes. And you don't have to do that."

"I like to keep busy, and I'll feel less guilty showing up here if I do something useful."

She scraped carrots and Daphne washed lettuce greens in her huge stainless sink, wondering how she could help this poor girl. But she'd set herself a nearly impossible task.

"The truth is, I don't think that anyone knows what inspires Scott, not even Scott until it happens. I could more easily tell you what to stay away from. He won't touch anywhere that's ever been a burial ground or a ceremonial spot for the native peoples."

"Right. I read an article where he came out against a developer that wanted to pave over a burial site."

Okay, so she hadn't been helpful there. She tried to think what else her son was passionate about. "He doesn't like to tear down perfectly sound buildings, he thinks it's wasteful. Um, he loves the idea of a completely self-sufficient house, so solar panels, water collection systems, abundant natural building materials." She shrugged. "You could find all this on the Internet." And that was the trouble with having a famous son. It was getting to the point where she sometimes went on the Internet if she wanted to keep up with him. Not that he wasn't a wonderful son, because he was. Kind and thoughtful, but he was also self-absorbed and forgetful.

"I'm sorry I can't be more help. My son and his girlfriend decided they wanted to get married here. Here!" She glanced around. Holly did the same. "Since they are keeping the wedding to family and close friends, and Evan's family is so big, it makes sense. But I don't know the first thing about planning a wedding." She gestured to the desk in the kitchen crowded with various brochures and scribbled notes.

Holly dried her hands and walked over to the desk. She started to reach for a photographer's glossy brochure then glanced up. "May I?"

Daphne nodded, wondering what on earth this woman was planning. And before her bemused gaze, Holly stacked, sorted and said, "What you need is a single place to keep all the wedding information. You could do it digitally, with a database." She glanced up at Daphne, obviously sensing that she was not the database type. "Or just get a binder and make sections for flowers, catering, photography, and so on. I can put it together for you."

"Holly, you might be an angel who flew in the door."

Her visitor laughed. "I have to work on a million projects at once for a difficult boss. I need to stay organized." She paused. "Plus, I'm really good at it."

Within half an hour, Holly had everything organized and sectioned, ready for a binder. "I'm sure you can buy ready-made wedding planners, but it would be just as easy to get a nice big three-ring binder and make your own."

Daphne got on the phone to Evan to ask him to pick one up on his way.

She turned to Holly. "This will be the first weekend I've had most of my children home in I don't know how long."

"Is Prescott coming here?" Holly's alarm showed in her heightened color and panic-struck eyes.

"Yes."

"Man, my timing sucks."

Or not, Daphne thought. Or not.

CHAPTER 4

Prescott rarely took a weekend off, but his big brother Evan was getting married in a few weeks and he wanted everyone to meet his bride. He also wanted his brothers as ushers or groomsmen or whatever you called them. In theory, Prescott didn't have a problem with this, and if he could simply show up and hang out with his family for the weekend of the wedding, meet the bride, dance with his mother and get back in his car and drive home, everything would be fine.

But, naturally, anything that simple wasn't nearly chaotic enough for his family. No. He was required to show up weeks before the wedding. Get measured for a rental tux. He had a perfectly good tuxedo hanging in his closet, hand made for him in Italy because he appreciated fine design in all things. But no. A hand-tailored tux wasn't acceptable to Evan. He insisted they all wear matching monkey suits from some god-awful rental place. That was bad enough. Worse, this dog and pony show required him to spend an entire weekend before the wedding caught up in a series of events that he suspected only God and Daphne Chance entirely grasped.

Prescott could appreciate that the first wedding of the Chance clan was a big deal to his mom. But did she have to force the rest of them into submission? Prescott liked Evan. He liked all his sibs fine in small doses, but he'd escaped the madness, the noise, the constant drama with a feeling of relief. Even the bad dreams had stopped. Now his life was calm, orderly, efficient.

But, as easygoing as Jack and Daphne Chance were, there were times when it was understood that everybody toed the line. This was one of those times.

The one good thing about getting out of town for the weekend was that it gave him a rest from Holly Legere, the woman who was increasingly bringing an element of chaos into his well-ordered life.

He liked her and didn't want her to lose her job, but he couldn't believe she'd talked him into looking at five sites. She didn't have a bad eye, either, but even if he'd wanted to design a home for a man like Rupert, which he didn't, he'd still need to find the right property. He'd come around to accepting that if she found him the right site, he'd have to live up to his word.

And once more he found himself trying to figure out when he'd gone from saying a definite no to Rupert to a qualified yes to Holly. It was madness.

But she looked at him with those appealing big eyes and he found himself wishing he could give her some money so she could get a decent job with a new company and a boss who appreciated her, but of course there was no way to do that without insulting her or—well, it was altogether too complicated. So his normal complete focus kept being interrupted by her, either in his thoughts or physically showing up in his office. He tried to pretend he didn't find her attractive, but he did. He'd dated much more beautiful women, but there was something about Holly that grabbed at him in a way that wasn't sensible at all. She was exactly the opposite of the kind of woman he liked. But he couldn't deny that he felt attracted to her energy and her intensity and her silly sense of humor. Not that he had any intention of acting on this strange and inconvenient feeling.

A weekend off was a really good idea.

For that peace of mind he might even consent to force himself into a rental tux that no doubt smelled of dry cleaning fluid and the last occupant's body odor.

As his Tesla purred along, quiet, efficient, a pleasure to all his senses, he wondered what he was going to do about Holly.

One good thing about going home was that if he could drag his mother away from wedding planning for half an hour, perhaps he could discuss the problem of Holly with her. There was no one like Daphne Chance for good advice when you were in a jam.

He thought back to some of the youthful exploits of the Chance kids and cracked a grin. Daphne had dealt with broken windows, broken hearts, inept drinking binges, broken bones, broken dreams, tears, tantrums and a couple of times, the law. She never, ever turned from the face of danger. She'd support her kids no matter what. But if you did wrong in her eyes, you would pay.

His grin shifted to a grimace as he recalled how many times he or one of his siblings—brothers, usually—had spent a much-longed-for Saturday weeding vegetable beds or mowing the vast acres of the Chance property. They'd apologized to mean neighbors, paid for new windows out of their meager pocket money and generally learned to walk the straight and narrow.

But in a tight spot? There was no one else he could imagine turning to than his mom and dad.

As his car ate up the miles, he wondered if he might be in a jam now.

His phone rang. He so rarely turned it on that the tone startled him. He clicked a button on the steering wheel when he saw it was his mother calling.

"Yes," he said without preamble. "I'm still coming. On my way."

"The best thing about a wedding is getting all my kids under one roof," she said, sounding thrilled with the whole insane enterprise.

"If I'm ever crazy enough to get married, I'll send you a postcard when the deed is done."

"Oh, Scott," she said, assuming he was joking. "Honey, I forgot to ask if you're bringing a date for the weekend?"

It was as well she couldn't see his face. He could not imagine anything that would entice him to subject a woman he was sleeping with to his family. He dated women who were quiet, elegant, who guarded their time, freedom and privacy as zealously as he did himself. His most recent girl-friend, Luigia, didn't even speak English. She spoke only Italian while he had exactly enough proficiency in that language to order a decent meal, give directions to a cab driver and greet a client. In some ways, their inability to talk to each other had helped the relationship. It hadn't ended because of a language barrier, but because he'd finished the project he'd taken on the Amalfi Coast. Neither of them had been committed enough to commute for the sake of seeing each other, so they'd parted with a final weekend on Capri and no hard feelings.

He tried to imagine bringing Luigia to the Chance family home in Hidden Falls and chuckled. No. He could safely assure his mother that he would not be bringing a date for the weekend.

He pulled into the big gravel driveway in front of the ramshackle house around five that evening. From the number of cars already jammed in there, most of his brothers and sisters were already here.

He parked door-banging distance from a dirty SUV that could have belonged to at least half his siblings. He got out of the car, stretched, breathed in the damp Oregon air and experienced a moment of satisfaction. He was home.

Strange to feel that way. He liked his life in San Francisco but, as crazy as it was, he supposed there was never going to be any place to beat this for making him feel nostalgic.

He removed his one case, wishing there were a decent hotel in or near Hidden Falls, and trod over the crushed gravel spotted with weeds to the front door.

Before he could knock, the door was flung open by his brother Cooper. Cooper was the youngest boy and even at twenty-six still reminded Prescott of an untrained puppy. He was bouncy, eager, in your face. Somebody needed to take a rolled newspaper to his nose.

"Scott, my man." He threw his arms around Prescott, who had no choice but to do an awkward man hug, his case still in one hand.

"You been holding out on us." Cooper sported a smirk that suggested he'd been making trouble or was thinking about it.

"I always hold out on you," Prescott reminded him. "Self-defense."

"No. I mean the hottie."

"Hottie?" One, he'd never use that term, and two, he'd never bring a woman he cared about to this madhouse.

"Seriously, way hotter than the stick-up-the-ass runway types you usually go for."

As Prescott was about to ask if his brother was high, his world turned sideways.

Holly Legere, the last person he'd have imagined, was walking down the hall behind where his brother was standing. She had the nervous stance of an interloper and was pushing her screwball curls behind her ears as though she could make them disappear. He'd only ever seen her in business wear but she wore a pair of well-worn jeans with a striped T-shirt and an ancient jean jacket. Her boots were scuffed.

So many questions crowded together on his tongue that he simply stood there, staring.

She walked up to stand beside Cooper, who held the door wider, a huge grin on his face. Holly said, "I had no idea you were coming this weekend."

He had a few things to say to Holly but he didn't want an audience. Particularly not Cooper.

"Could we have a moment?" he asked his youngest brother.

And in typical youngest brother fashion, Cooper whined. "I always miss everything." But he did take Prescott's case out of his hand and disappeared inside the house with it.

Holly stepped out to where Prescott was still standing, stupefied, and she shut the door behind her.

Since it was obvious his first question would be 'What the hell are you doing here?' he didn't bother voicing it. Holly, in his experience, wasn't one to let silence lengthen.

"I am so sorry," she said. "I—" She tilted her head back

as though God might write a script for her on the sky. "I've heard you talk about your mom a few times and I thought maybe if I talked to her, I could get a clue into how to reach you."

"You had no right."

She looked at him then and instead of hanging her head, she raised it in challenge. "I think I had a right to ask your mom if she'd talk to me, to see if she had any insights into the kind of property that might appeal to you. And she had a right to say no." She shrugged. She didn't admit that his mother had talked to her, but since she had come from inside the house, it seemed likely.

He began to see the humor in the situation. He'd planned to talk to his mother about Holly and she'd beaten him here, to talk to his mother about him.

"And what did she say to you?"

"Nothing. Your mother is one of the nicest people I've ever met. But mostly she let me do the talking."

His chest eased and he realized he should have had more faith in his mom. She wouldn't talk about him behind his back. But it sounded very much like Daphne to let Holly unload all her problems onto shoulders that had carried plenty in her time.

"Don't you have parents of your own you can talk to?"

She blinked at him, her green eyes widening. "Prescott Chance, that is the first personal question you have ever asked me."

And didn't that just figure? Two minutes home and he was falling into the Chance way. Madness and chaos and finding out way too much about people that you didn't need to know. And didn't Holly fit right in?

As he was about to ask if she needed help packing her car, the door opened once more and there was his mother.

Daphne was still an eyeful even in her mid fifties. She had a yurt in the back yard that Jack had put up for her. In it she practiced yoga and mediation every day. Maybe that's what kept her looking so young. She wore snug black yoga pants and a shirt patterned with yin and yang symbols.

Maybe there was a little more gray in her hair than last time he'd seen her, but not much.

Her eyes were still as blue, her smile as warm. "Scott," she said as she ran out to give him a hug, squeezing tight so he had to laugh and pull back.

"You'll break a rib."

"I'm just so happy you're here. You're all here."

He felt himself going pale. "All here?"

"Most of you." She was so happy her eyes were a little wet. "Having all my children together again. That hasn't happened in years."

And please God it didn't happen again anytime soon.

"Holly arrived like an angel here to answer my prayers. She has been a lifesaver."

He felt his eyes widening. But he noticed Holly's eyes widening too.

"Really?"

"Yes. When she arrived I was desperate about the wedding venue. But she figured it all out."

"Wedding venue?" What on earth was she talking about?

"Yes. Evan and Caitlyn want to have the wedding right here, which is wonderful, but they're getting married in October. How do you plan for the weather? It could be sunny and warm or cold and rainy. Plus, this house isn't exactly fancy. But Holly walked around the property and we figured out exactly where we could put a big tent and get some of those portable heaters like in restaurants. And she's got some terrific ideas about using potted trees to block out anything unsightly in the background. She believes we can create a fairy tale oasis right here."

"A fairy tale oasis." Good Lord. But even as part of him rebelled, his working brain was already thinking he'd have to take a look at the lawn in question. He wondered if they'd need to work up some kind of raised platform to support tables and prevent the guests dancing in mud. Maybe he could rig something. Figure out some kind of siding that would keep the cold and rain out but let the light in so you kept the idea of a garden wedding even if the weather didn't cooperate. He had staff with all kinds of expertise. He'd make a note to ask.

His mother seemed so happy. "She said she's an assistant to Alistair Rupert. No wonder she's so efficient."

"No wonder."

Holly said, "I'm good at planning things, that's all."

"It's too far for Holly to drive all the way back to San Francisco tonight, honey. I invited her to stay."

Oh, she had, had she?

His mom beamed at him. "But she's refusing. She says she'll drive back to Portland and get a hotel room. I'll leave it to you two to sort out."

And with another quick hug she was gone.

"Really," Holly said, looking embarrassed and harassed and hot. "I'm fine staying in a hotel. This is a family thing. Honestly Prescott, if I'd have any idea..."

Of course he'd planned to pack her on out of there before he so much as stepped into the family home. And now, no sooner did she tell him that she'd get herself a hotel than he recalled all the things she'd told him. She claimed he'd never asked her a personal question, which was likely true. He didn't need to. She was always so busy talking that he knew quite a lot about her. How she worked for slave wages and only stayed with Rupert so she could pay off her student loans. One night in Portland for her was probably equivalent to him spending a month at the George V in Paris.

Besides, he could see the smudged blue shadows under her eyes that denoted fatigue. He didn't want her driving a couple of hours.

"Why don't you stay tonight? You can head off in the morning."

"I don't want to be in the way."

He grinned suddenly. "In this family? You have to work at it to be noticed."

Still, she looked unsure.

"Please," he heard himself say. "I want you to." And what the hell was that about? But as he spoke the words, he realized they were true. Weirdly, he thought he'd enjoy having her here.

She sighed. "It would be really nice not to have to get into my car again."

"Okay, then. It's settled."

Before they got to the front door, she stopped him with a hand on his arm. "I didn't know," she said. There was appeal swimming in her sea green eyes.

There were women calculating enough to have tracked his movements and arranged this accidental meeting. He'd never known such people existed until he'd been named to a list of America's most eligible bachelors and he'd discovered there were women who hunted men like him. He'd found the scheming sometimes flattering, occasionally disturbing, but he'd never been remotely interested in any of the women who put themselves in his way in a calculated move.

First, he didn't want to be a catch.

Even more, he didn't want to be caught.

He knew in his bones that Holly was not one of those women. He felt the pressure of her hand on his arm, felt the warmth coming through his sleeve. He was tempted to put his hand over hers, to let her know it was okay.

She started like a hornet had stung her and at that moment he heard the drone of her cell phone. She had it on vibrate but he could hear the jarring noise, already feel it splitting her attention.

She dropped his arm, fumbled in her pocket and turned it off, but not before he regretted his weakness in telling her she could stay.

He stared down at her. "One rule."

"Don't say it," she begged as though she'd read his mind.

"No cell phones."

Her eyes did the big wide innocent thing. "I'll lose my job."

"It's the weekend," he reminded her.

She pushed back that hopeless mass of curls. "Slaves don't get weekends. We work 24/7."

He wasn't an unreasonable man. He'd already gone way out of his way to ensure she didn't lose a job that seemed to be sucking her of energy. People said he was single minded, but he could compromise. "You may have cell phone access once every day for one hour," he decided.

"One hour?"

"Yes."

"But..."

"Take it or leave it."

She narrowed her eyes. "Which hour?"

"When I go for my run."

"Fine," she snapped. "I'll be in in a minute."

They both knew she was getting on that cell phone the

second he walked into the house. He could change his mind and set her on her way right now, but then he'd have his mother to deal with. He decided to ignore her current call.

As he was entering the house, he heard her say in a low voice, but not nearly low enough, "I'm caught between two egomaniacs. Kill me now."

CHAPTER 5

Then he walked into his house and was enveloped by the madness that both repelled him and that had helped shape him.

Jack and Daphne Chance were remarkable people. They'd met when a nineteen-year old Daphne was pregnant with another man's child. They'd married and had kids of their own. They also picked up strays along the way. They wouldn't turn away a child whose parents were unable or unwilling to provide a loving home. Over the years, they'd ended up with eleven. One of the many things he admired about his folks was that they refused to differentiate between the kids who were adopted and those who weren't. Jack, a foster kid with some bitter memories, said he never wanted to be one of those men who announced, "This is my son so and so and my adopted son, such and such."

The deal was that when the kids reached sixteen they could ask if they wanted to find out the truth of their parentage. Of course, the older ones had a pretty good idea about the ancestry of the younger ones, but they'd grown up understanding that keeping that secret was an unbreakable family deal.

He had some murky memories of his own origins but sixteen had come and gone and he'd found he didn't really care. He strongly suspected he did not spring from the loins of Jack and Daphne. Based on his dark looks and a certain affinity he felt for the land, he believed he was part native. He had never said those words aloud, but some journalist somewhere had suggested that he was a shaman. The idea had stuck and been repeated so often it was part of his professional aura. He never confirmed or denied. Frankly, he didn't know.

And the last thing he wanted to do was dig into his beginnings. Some things were better left buried.

He headed toward the low roar coming from the living room and found most of his family gathered together.

In the pandemonium that greeted his arrival, Evan finally yelled louder than anyone else, which was pretty much how you got people's attention in the Chance household. "Guys, hold up, I gotta introduce Prescott to Caitlyn."

A grinning Evan came forward looking happier and more at home with himself than Prescott had ever seen him. "Scott, this is the woman who is planning to join the family, so behave yourself."

He fell in love with his soon-to-be sister-in-law on sight. She was gorgeous, elegant, but also had a warmth that most of Evan's previous girls had lacked.

She rose and they shook hands. "I'm so happy to meet you," she said with a refined East Coast accent.

"Sorry we haven't met sooner." He'd been so busy with work. Always work. That was his excuse, anyway. But now that he was here he was conscious that he'd missed his sibs.

He glanced around the crowded living room.

All of them were there but one.

"Where's Ben?" Ben was the oldest and the one who was home least. The family rule about keeping a person's parentage secret didn't apply to him. Since he was half black, it was pretty obvious Jack wasn't his father.

"He's on some kind of hush-hush government business."

For a while they'd all thought Ben was a spy, but it turned out he was involved in trade talks. Hush-hush because of global economic rather than political or military reasons, though, of course, the economy connected to all of it.

While he chatted with Caitlyn, he saw Holly enter his peripheral vision. She paused, hovered at the edge of things, still appearing a little unsure of her welcome.

"Did everybody meet Holly?" he yelled in his turn, drawing her into the room.

Since she'd arrived at his home before him, it seemed like everybody had.

He pulled her forward by the hand and found her a seat by kicking Cooper off his.

"Oh, no, that's okay," she said when he gave Cooper the heave-ho.

"I'm used to it," Cooper said with good nature. "Been abused all my life."

He could feel the curiosity pulsing as they all tried to figure out his relationship with Holly. Even Cooper, who could usually be relied upon to ask the awkward question, was strangely silent. Finally, he said, "Holly and I work together."

"Oh," about three people said at once, in various tones of *Then what's she doing at our family home on a weekend?*

None of anyone's business so he left it at that and engaged Caitlyn in conversation, keeping Holly included.

Since Prescott didn't believe idle conversation served a purpose, he got right to a subject that concerned him. "Evan isn't really going to make us all wear rented tuxes, is he?"

Caitlyn seemed like a sensible woman, and everyone knew the bride was the one who made all the critical decisions about a wedding. Also, he could tell from one look at her that she had class and good taste. He felt he could count on her.

"Oh, well." She pushed her long hair behind her ears in a gesture that made her look like a high school student and not an accomplished doctor in her thirties. She glanced to Evan in appeal. "That's really not my decision."

Evan must have sensed what was going on for he came over and sat on the floor at Caitlyn's feet. "What's my little brother doing now?" he asked as though Prescott had borrowed his car without asking. Honestly, it had only happened that once. Prescott was still proud that he hadn't hurt the deer that had leapt in front of him on the highway and only the car was totaled. Evan, however, hadn't seen it that way, and a backyard brawl culminating in a painful black eye had ensued.

"I'm trying to talk your girlfriend, who seems like a woman of taste, out of those awful tuxes. We'll look like the Osmond Brothers."

"But way better looking," Evan insisted.

"Cooper?" he appealed.

"Hey, anything that's not a hand-me-down is good for me." He loved to claim that he'd only ever worn clothes each of his brothers had worn before him. It wasn't true. Mostly.

Realizing that he wasn't going to get anything but grief from pushing the issue with the tuxes, he went to work on the next item on his agenda.

He cornered his mom in the kitchen on the pretext of helping with dinner. "Where are you putting Holly?" he asked, thinking the house was going to burst at the seams with all of them home. It had been bad enough when they were kids and smaller, but now there were eleven adults, plus guests, plus Jack and Daphne. He couldn't imagine where she was going to stash everybody.

His mother opened the oven and a burst of steam hit her in the face. She backed away and then started to ease out a huge pan of lasagna. He pushed her out of the way and took the pot holders from her. Then he muscled the massive casserole onto the wooden block counter. Jack had built it and Prescott could see where the nails hadn't been properly countersunk.

"I had to put her in your room, honey. The girls' rooms are all full. Obviously, I had to give Evan and Caitlyn the guest cottage. There's nowhere else."

It was the room he and Evan had shared as kids. He narrowed his eyes at her. "Are there still bunk beds in there?"

She puffed out a breath. "What else do you suggest?"

"Mom, why don't you let me design you and dad a new house? Something with room for everybody and more bathrooms? I've got more money than I can ever spend. I'd like to do it."

She patted his cheek and smiled her warm mom smile. "You are such a dear. But as crazy as this old place is, it's where I've lived since I first got married. Your dad's added on as our family grew and a lot of love went into the place.

Also a lot of crooked nails since Jack was a more enthusiastic home renovator than a talented one.

Before he could say more, Holly walked into the kitchen. "Can I help?"

Then she spied the enormous lasagna. "Oh, that smells fantastic."

"It's the same recipe I've been making for years. Everybody loves it."

Prescott opened the fridge and pulled out the salad he knew he'd find in there. "Listen, Holly, my mom had to put us in the same room since we're full to the rafters with Chance kids." He winced thinking of his custom-designed bedroom and the spa-like en suite in his apartment. "It's bunk beds."

She blushed a little. "Oh. I hadn't realized. Um, is that okay with you?"

None of this was okay with him.

He still had no idea how he'd ended up in this mess. And sharing his bunk-bed room with a girl seemed like the final indignity. Maybe it wouldn't matter so much if there wasn't this unwilling attraction that he suspected she felt too.

"Of course we want you to stay," his mother insisted, seemingly oblivious to the undercurrent. "Marguerite's got night things you can borrow and I always have extra toothbrushes and so on."

But Holly bit her lip and looked at him.

What could he do?

He leveled a tough guy look her way. "I get the top bunk," he said.

Then she grinned at him and he noticed how pretty she was when she wasn't worrying about pleasing Alistair Rupert or doing a million things all at the same time.

"Deal," she said.

∼

You learned a lot about a man from the way he behaved with his family, Holly thought. With the Chances it was closer to a tribe than a family because there were so many of them. The girls mainly had flower names so it was hard to keep them straight, but Holly was doing her best. The boys, well, men she supposed though it seemed they all acted like boys when they got together, were like a rolling mass of puppies. She couldn't begin to tell them apart.

She had a sense that when the full brood got together all of them fell back in time so she had a picture of what Prescott would have been like as a boy.

Everybody sat at a long table that reminded her of those in her college cafeteria, except that it was clear everyone had assigned seating, and she'd been shoehorned in between a brother whose name was James, a nice-looking guy with military short hair and a charming smile, and Iris's boyfriend, a nice guy, the local high school English teacher. His name was Geoff.

Prescott carried out what had to be the world's largest pan of lasagna, and Daphne followed with the salad Holly had helped her make.

Jack Chance, bearded and beaming, came in carrying a huge glass jug of red wine. "My latest vintage," he said proudly.

Geoff leaned close. "A word of warning," he said, "one outsider to another. That stuff will strip paint. Beware."

"Thanks," she whispered back.

Jack slopped wine into glasses. She knew from her research that Prescott had fine tastes in everything and she'd have included wine in that category, but he accepted the garnet-colored brew.

And sipped water.

And then she got it. Nobody wanted to hurt Jack

Chance's feelings. She imagined they'd drink a little and the rest would get chucked out and their dad would never know the difference.

A rush of affection filled her.

In her turn she accepted a glass of wine.

Meanwhile, Daphne was dishing up lasagna, handing the plates off to . . .was that Marguerite? Who was adding a spoon of salad to each one.

Then the plates were passed along.

When they'd all been served, Jack raised his glass. "I want to propose a toast," he said. He looked like a man happy with his life, proud of his brood, at peace with the world. His cheeks were ruddy, his beard more gray than brown, but his blue eyes still twinkled with youth. "I want to thank all of you for coming home to celebrate the first wedding in our family. And I want to thank Caitlyn for agreeing to join our crazy brood. A man gets to an age when he realizes his best days are behind him. But I look around me and I see that my life has real meaning. Daphne," he said, looking down the table to his wife at the other end. "We've got a beautiful family." His voice grew husky but he seemed perfectly comfortable with his own emotions. "I am proud of every one of you, proud of who you've all become. I thank God every day for my wife, and my family."

There were a couple of sniffles from around the table and Holly felt her own eyes grow moist.

"Evan, you've chosen well, son, and on behalf of all of us, I wish you both as happy a marriage as Daphne and I have enjoyed."

"Oh, Jack," Daphne said. And she got right up out of her chair and walked around the table to give him a kiss.

Holly wondered what it would feel like to have a man love her that much, to feel that kind of satisfaction with life.

Of its own volition, her gaze shifted to Prescott. He always seemed so remote to her. So self-contained. To her surprise, she saw him smiling at the kissing going on at the end of the table, looking for a second as though he might actually be human.

"Okay, guys," he finally called out. "Knock it off in front of the children. This is a PG dinner."

With a laugh, Daphne hauled herself off her husband's lap. When she'd returned to her seat, she said, "I want to echo everything Jack said." She turned to Caitlyn. "Caitlyn, honey, welcome to the Chance family."

They all drank a toast and Holly immediately understood what Geoff had meant. As the wine hit her tongue her entire mouth felt like it was being scrubbed out with a scouring pad.

Fortunately, the large water glasses were full. The lasagna tasted as good as it smelled. The salad was similarly wonderful. She ate on such a tight budget that she could never afford the fancy greens in the market. "Oh, this salad is so good," she said.

"Thank you, honey. Marguerite's our green thumb."

Holly was astonished. "You grew this?"

"Sure. I have a house on the property. Come over tomorrow and I'll give you a tour of the organic veggie farm. I sell most of it to restaurants and at a farmers' market, and the rest we eat ourselves."

"I can't tell you the last time I ate a salad that didn't come in a bag," she admitted. Usually marked down, but she didn't bother sharing that fact.

James called across the table to his sister, "How's the coffee shop doing, Iris? Since you opened the second location?"

She'd already been told that Iris owned the best bakery café in town. But Holly didn't know she'd franchised. Cool.

As Holly began to listen to Iris talk about how her assistant had pretty much taken on the everyday management of the new location, up at the other end of the table, Evan asked Cooper how his exams were coming. Cooper was getting his Ph.D. in some field of genetics. She was interested in that, too, and tried to listen to both conversations at once. But then Jack asked James about a big Seattle drug bust that he'd seen on the TV news.

James, she soon realized, was a cop in Seattle.

She discovered that a conversation around the Chance household was more like a brush fire. New blazes would spring up everywhere and there was no way to stay on top of them all.

Her own family had always been more of the children should be seen and not heard model, and her folks didn't have a whole lot to say to each other so family dinners had been pretty silent. Her dad was Irish, her mom from Kansas, and they'd met on a blind date when he was newly in the country. She thought that the Irish lad had been homesick and her mother had been attracted by how different he was from the other boys she knew. Because it wasn't like they had anything in common. The fact that they were still together was more from habit than affection.

She had a brother, Aidan, in the army, posted to Germany, so she rarely saw him. She made a duty phone call to her mom every week, and sometimes they ran out of things to say.

Nobody here seemed to have that problem. They were all interested in each other's lives. Seemed to genuinely like each other.

Holly felt as though she'd stepped out of a cold room and into the sun.

Ouch, she thought, as she scooped up another flavorful bite of lasagna. Bad metaphor. Corny and self involved.

But she did like the Chances. She liked them a lot.

She'd imagined Prescott coming from a cold, upper-class family somewhere. She'd never believed the mythology surrounding him that he was a shaman. The very fact that he never talked about his background had suggested to her right away, when she was studying his life as though there'd be a final exam, that he'd come from some entirely uninteresting background.

The truth was so much more.

"Are they always like this?" she asked Geoff.

"Everybody talking at once and the noise level rising by the second?"

She nodded.

He grinned at her. "Pretty much. You get used to it after a while." He seemed to realize that he was making assumptions and shifted in his chair. "If you stick around."

This crowd was noisy, barely controlled and lovable. And among them, she saw a Prescott she'd never have believed existed. Funny, warm, maybe not as talkative as the rest of them, but he wasn't off somewhere in the dark hanging upside down, either, which she'd suspected he did in his spare time.

As though he felt her watching him, Prescott's gaze suddenly connected with hers, too fast for her to look away.

He didn't smile at her, exactly, but his expression softened and she felt that he'd forgiven her for showing up on the very weekend when his entire family would be here. When she smiled back at him, she felt something more. A warmth that had begun to build. She didn't want to be attracted to a man who was known for dating the hottest women on the planet. Nothing could come of it but heartbreak, and yet, when he looked at her this way she couldn't resist the pull.

~

After dinner everybody fell into the prescribed roles as though none of them had ever left home. Dishes were scraped, stacked, passed along. You cleared or you loaded the dishwasher, or you washed or dried and put away. Both Holly and Caitlyn tried to pitch in but Daphne waved them into the living room. "Holly, tell Caitlyn about some of your ideas for the wedding," she said. "I'll bring coffee through in a minute."

Prescott couldn't imagine what Holly could add to wedding planning but he wasn't one to let opportunity slip by. As he walked by her, ostensibly to collect napkins from the table, he said, "Try to talk her out of the rental tuxes."

Before she could answer, Caitlyn took Holly by the hand and pulled her toward the living room. "Daphne says you're a genius at organization. And you have some ideas."

Good. He hoped she came up with a better idea than matching tuxes.

Prescott did not bring women home. Never had. He'd always shuddered at the thought of trying to explain the mess and the dog hair and the yurt. At the voices all talking at once, the in jokes, the shorthand that developed when you have that many people in one house.

But, as they all relaxed over coffee in the living room, he glanced over at Holly and saw her laughing at something James was saying to her. It occurred to him that she was having no trouble keeping up. Maybe she didn't catch all the in jokes, but she didn't seem to mind. And instead of being horrified by dog hair, she was sitting on the ground with Lucky's head on her knee. The dog wore a totally blissed-out canine grin on her face as Holly pulled gently on her ears. A second dog, Henry, some kind of terrier who'd been clobbered with the ugly brick, flopped on the floor at Evan's feet.

They settled into groups as usually happened. There were just too many of them to have a single conversation. Because it had been so long since he'd been home, Prescott made an effort to chat with every one of his sibs. And from his peripheral vision he kept an eye on Holly. Not that she needed rescuing. She was no wallflower. Both James and Cooper seemed determined to make her laugh, and she was happy to oblige. She had a great laugh. Low and husky.

As he moved around, he talked first to Paisley, the baby of the family, who he hardly knew since there were twelve years between them. She was growing into a very pretty woman. She must be twenty-two now and a college student. She made a point of telling him how much she liked Holly.

He moved on to Lauren. Lauren was the official hottie in the family. He thought all his sisters were good looking, but Lauren was the kind of woman who got poetry and love songs written to her. Instead of making her stuck up and obnoxious, though, the constant attention had made her pull into herself a little bit. She tried to disguise her crazy beauty, which somehow only made her more attractive. "How's it going, little sis?" he asked, sitting beside her.

"Okay. But I'd forgotten how noisy it gets with all of us here."

"I know. Wish I'd brought ear plugs."

She smiled. "And with the plus ones, the place is bursting at the seams."

He put up his hands. "Hey, Holly and I might be involved in a project together, that's all."

"I like her," was all she said.

Rose and Marguerite made sure he knew how much they liked Holly, too.

Since every single brother and sister made some comment about how much they liked Holly he decided to be absolutely clear to all of them—Holly included—that nothing was going on between him and Alistair Rupert's assistant. So, when it got to bedtime, he challenged his dad to a game of crib. When Holly headed off to the bunk room with a slightly shy, "Good night," he was deep into a game. By the time he and Jack had played three games and managed to discuss everything from local politics to sports to how happy he was that Evan had found a great girl, it was well after midnight.

They packed up the game and Prescott undressed in the bathroom before slipping into the bunkroom. Holly was a softly breathing shape on the bottom bunk. She'd left a lamp burning for him, and as he flicked it off, she stirred.

"G'night," she said sleepily.

"Good night." He climbed up the ladder and into the bunk bed. And, since he was thirty-four and had gained a few inches since he'd last slept in here, he banged his head on the ceiling getting in.

THE DINNER GONG, which Daphne had bought at a flea market when they were young, clanged, waking Prescott. To his relief, his bunkmate was long gone, leaving nothing but a neatly made bunk bed and the slight scent of wildflowers.

She was already seated at the table when he wandered

out to the kitchen to hit the coffee pot. She wore the same clothes she'd arrived in, and she smiled shyly when he said good morning.

Breakfast was farm fresh eggs, an enormous plate of bacon, skyscrapers of toast and pancakes as well as yogurt and fruit for anyone who hoped to keep their arteries clear.

"Don't forget everybody, the tux fitting's at noon," Evan announced.

Prescott shuddered and drank more coffee.

"And we girls will do some wedding planning," Daphne said, sounding like it was the most exciting thing she'd ever done in her life. "And we have to address all the envelopes for the wedding invitations."

Holly happily accepted another pancake from James and poured maple syrup liberally. "This is so good," she said, munching happily.

When breakfast was done and cleaned up, she said, "Well, I should really get going. I've got a long drive."

It wasn't his mother who stopped her this time. It was Caitlyn. "Oh, no, please. You can't go already. I loved your ideas for the wedding. I was hoping you could help us plan it all. I have so little time, I need to get everything nailed down this weekend." Caitlyn didn't seem like someone who was comfortable asking for things, so she must really want Holly's help.

Holly glanced at him helplessly, but what was he supposed to do? Kick her out? "Hey," he said, holding up his hands. "Knock yourself out."

"Well, okay, then. Thanks. I'd love to help." The strange thing was that she genuinely did seem like she wanted to give herself writer's cramp addressing invitations to Caitlyn and Evan's wedding.

"So," James said, as soon as it was settled that she was

staying. "Do you want to see the first house Scott ever designed?"

Prescott's first design was generally accepted to be an energy neutral home he'd designed after winning a prestigious contest back in his twenties. The house nestled on a wooded hilltop outside Seattle. Somehow, he did not think James was planning to take their guest there.

She nodded, looking thrilled, and the two scrambled to their feet. Lucky jumped up to follow, tail swishing. Henry, not to be left out, jumped to his stubby little legs and shook himself before trotting along behind. Prescott had a pretty good idea where they were headed. He watched them out of the big picture window and, sure enough, saw them head past the pond. He toyed with remaining where he was and then strode outside to follow.

As James must have known he'd do, for when he arrived at the spot, his little brother was putting on a spiel as though he were a TV announcer on one of those home and garden shows. "You'll notice the radiant heating from the thermal-paned windows and the tilt of the cantilevered roof. Many people consider the Gestalt House to be Prescott's first home design, but we here in Hidden Falls lay claim to his very first design."

He thrust his hand dramatically in the air to where a rickety set of boards had been nailed into a tree trunk. "The Tree house."

Holly laughed, but then she laughed at pretty much everything James said.

Then, to his surprise, she backed up and stared at that foolish tree fort he'd built when he was a kid as though she was taking James seriously.

"Holly," he said, "it really is just a tree house. I built it when I was a kid."

Still, she remained staring up at it, moving sideways to get a different view. "You know, every tree house I've ever seen is pretty much the same. A few boards nailed down and plywood walls and a roof. But this, this actually looks interesting. You can see a creative mind at work."

He'd scrounged around in the barn and found some old windows and the bits and pieces of timber that his dad always had lying around. He remembered cutting down an old door and remaking it to fit. All he had by way of carpentry skills were what he'd learned from his dad and then learned properly in a high school course. As crude as it was, the structure still looked pretty solid, twenty years later.

She walked halfway around the old oak and back again. "You made the house fit the tree instead of sticking a house shape in there like most people would." She turned back to him. "Is that when you knew what you wanted to be when you grew up?"

Was it? He could remember to this day the fun he'd had drawing and redrawing his plans, the pencil sketches on graph paper, the way he'd wanted to capture the sun and keep out the rain. He shrugged. "Who knows?'

She was about to speak and then something beeped. Before he could remind her about their deal, she said, "That is not a cell phone. I set a reminder. I have to go help your mom and Caitlyn. We're talking about table decorations. And then she ran off, Lucky following her like a shaggy shadow. Henry looked at the retreating Holly, back to Prescott and James, sneezed once, then trotted after Holly and Lucky.

Table decorations? What the hell was his mother doing getting Holly involved in table decorations? Couldn't she see that Holly was overscheduled and overworked as it was? Could she not have one weekend off?

"She's a fun girl," James said.

"Yes. She is."

His younger brother glanced sideways at him. "Hot, too."

"Maybe, but not my type."

James grinned. "I was hoping you'd say that."

"Why?"

He got a slap on the back, buddy to buddy, "Cause she's totally my type."

As his younger brother strode away after Holly, Prescott had the sudden urge to tackle his kid brother and wrestle him to the ground. He'd actually started to move when he caught himself. What the hell was he doing?

His brother was joking.

Had to be. Sure, James and Holly were around the same age, but he could not see the two of them together. If he tried, the picture wouldn't form.

CHAPTER 6

*P*rescott tried right up until the second they were leaving for the tux fittings to get out of having to dress in a rented tux.

But nobody supported him.

Nobody.

Not even his own mother, who patted him on the shoulder while clearly distracted by flower arrangements. "Nobody's going to look at you, darling. It's Evan's big day." Which effectively made him feel like he was acting like a childish oaf.

Not even his gay brother, who was the only person in the family who dressed better than Prescott himself. "It's a big deal to our brother," Josh said. "We'll have to suck it up."

All the men of the wedding party—and that was all the men except Ben—headed off. His father drove the ancient Volvo he refused to upgrade in spite of the rust holes in the door and the noise it made.

A few of them piled into that.

A few more piled into Evan's SUV. Prescott strode to his

Tesla, James by his side. James had won a noisy argument about who was riding shotgun in the fancy rig.

"Oh, man, this is amazing," James said as the car purred along as close to silent as you could get accounting for road noise.

James might be a pain in the ass little brother, but he knew engines. Soon they were talking cars and engine design. For a while he forgot the torture ahead.

Of course, being as they lived in Hidden Falls, which was pretty well named since it was hidden from most amenities, they drove almost an hour to a strip mall that housed Gents with Cents. As they pulled in front of the store front, which featured a display that was clearly aimed at young men heading to high school or college graduation, he realized they rented all kinds of clothing.

"Gents with Cents? Seriously?"

James turned to him, a frown creasing his brow. "Come on, Scott. I know you're a big shot but Cooper doesn't have any money." He held up his hand before Prescott could offer to buy their youngest student-brother his own tux. "And don't even think about offering to pay for his tux. He doesn't want charity."

Prescott didn't want to wear a rented tux, but no one seemed to take his feelings into consideration. But if his brother wanted to make him feel guilty, he was doing a good job.

"Come on," James said. "It's one day out of your life. Wear the crappy rental tux and make your brother happy."

"If I ever get married, I'm eloping."

He thought James might have muttered, "Good," but it was hard to be certain since they were climbing out of the car at the time.

As the Chance men walked into the rental place they crowded the small space.

The guy in charge, who looked like they might have caught him napping, or maybe watching YouTube, jumped to his feet from behind a counter. Evan stepped forward. "I'm Evan Chance. Do you remember me?"

"You betcha, Evan," he said, leaning forward to shake hands. "I've got everything ready for you."

"Great."

Prescott took a whiff of the place and felt his skin start to itch. But James's words had shamed him. When had he turned into such a dick? If his brother wanted him to dress up like Bozo the Clown for the wedding, he supposed he'd do it. Though, privately, he thought that Evan had been living in Hicksville too long. There was a time, back when he'd been a hotshot corporate lawyer charging an eye-popping hourly rate, when he'd have turned up his nose at a rental tux a lot faster than Prescott.

"Oh, these are great," Cooper said, checking out the racks of suits and tuxes. There was everything from traditional morning suits, if you wanted to fake being British aristocracy on your wedding day, to white polyester if your taste ran more to Trailer Park Boys.

You wanted an Elvis-themed wedding? Tropical? Cummerbunds to match any possible bridal color? Gents with Cents was your go-to establishment.

The old guy, who told them his name was Ed, banged around on his computer. "Ah, yes," he said. "You phoned ahead with all your approximate measurements."

He walked behind him to where a line of tuxes were all waiting on a rack.

Prescott blinked.

They were blue.

Not a navy, manly blue, either.

More of a powder blue.

Ed pulled out two of the matching tuxes. Walked over to his list. "Let's see, Cooper, this one's for you."

"Cool," said his utterly tasteless younger brother as he took the tux.

"There are two changing cubicles. You'll have to go in pairs, and then while we're getting the sizes right, getting the pants to the right length, the next two can go in."

He groaned inwardly. This was going to take all day.

"And Prescott," Ed said, holding out the second suit. "This should be your size."

With James's words still ringing in his ear he didn't say a word, simply grabbed the tux and headed for the change room.

Outside, he could hear them talking.

He stripped rapidly, pushing himself into the tux as fast as possible and hoping to be out of it again ASAP. Fortunately, there was no mirror in the changing room, but even looking down at his pale blue-covered legs made him queasy.

He had to give himself a quick pep talk, reminding himself once more that he was doing this for his brother. He took a deep breath, yanked back the curtain and marched out, a vision in powder blue.

When he walked out, he heard the click of cameras. Then a roar of laughter hit him like a wave crashing down on a surfer too stupid to see it coming.

"Punked!" Cooper yelled, high fiving Evan, who was laughing so hard he had to bend over.

As he stared at all his brothers and his father laughing themselves into snorts and coughing fits, he realized he'd been gone way too long not to have realized right away that he'd been set up.

"I am going to pound you senseless," he warned, advancing on the bridegroom who yelled, "Wait, I gotta upload this to Facebook."

Then he caught a glimpse of himself in the long mirror and, surrounded by the rest of the men in his family looking as normal as they could ever look, he was struck by how ridiculous he appeared.

"You look like Elvis in Vegas," Josh said, still chuckling.

And damn, now that this stunt had been pulled, it could never be pulled again.

He posed for another photo with all of them together, including Ed, and him standing proudly in the center.

Then he got out of the tux, knowing that being made a fool of was still better than wearing a powder blue tux for the wedding.

It turned out Evan was picking up a suit for Caitlyn's nephew, who was going to be a ring bearer.

As they left, Evan clapped Prescott on the back. "One day I knew I'd get even with you for totaling my car."

"Great. So, we're even?"

"How bout I drive the Tesla home?"

"Not a chance in hell."

He got another thump on the back. "Come on, I'm treating you all to lunch."

"So, what will we be wearing for the wedding?" Before he let his relief take over, he felt he'd like to know.

"Scott, it's an outdoor wedding in the back yard. We want everyone feeling relaxed and enjoying themselves. Wear whatever you want."

"Seriously?"

"Yeah."

He narrowed his gaze. "And those pictures you took?" He didn't for one second think his brother would upload them to a social media site. Okay, maybe for one second.

Evan laughed. Patted his smartphone. "One day I'll need a favor."

"That's blackmail."

"Yes, my friend, that's exactly what it is."

AFTER SOME GOOD male bonding in a sports bar, the cavalcade headed back to Hidden Falls. In the couple of hours they'd been gone, the threatening gray skies had moved beyond threat to actual rain.

Maybe his adopted city had to deal with fog, but he'd take that any day over the rain.

When he pulled into his parents' place it occurred to him suddenly that he'd even tried to get Holly to side with him about the tux rentals and she had spouted the "Suck it up, Prescott" family line.

He turned to James. "Did Holly know the tux place was a set up?"

"Yeah. We needed her to help talk you into it."

He walked into wedding planning central. Didn't people hire professionals for this sort of thing? His mom was talking to Iris about canapés. Canapés! And his sister was taking notes, which made him suspect that the Sunflower Coffee and Tea Company was branching out into wedding catering. At least for this wedding.

"Can't Evan and Caitlyn hire people to do this stuff?"

His mother and sister both turned identical stunned expressions his way. "Of course they can," his mother said.

"But we want to do it," Iris chimed in.

Whatever. He glanced around. "Where's Holly?"

"I'm not sure," his mom said, glancing around the big kitchen as though Holly might be lurking in a corner. "She was working on the wedding guest database last time I saw her. Oh, Scott, what that woman can do with a computer."

Wedding guest database? He felt a little irked on Holly's behalf. She worked so hard all week for that asshat. She shouldn't be stuck working all weekend on a wedding she wouldn't be attending for people she barely knew.

He strode out, thinking he'd take her for a drive or something, give her a break from the madness. It didn't take five minutes for the men in the family to hunker down in front of the big-screen TV in the living room for a football game.

He watched for a couple of minutes then went to find Holly. She wasn't in the house.

Neither was Lucky. Henry snoozed under Evan's chair, clearly not interested in going out in this weather.

Grabbing a rain jacket that likely belonged to his dad, he pushed out the back door and into the rain. No wonder Lucky was besotted if she'd found someone who'd take her for a walk in the rain.

He pulled up the hood, feeling the cold drops splash off him. It was sort of peaceful out here. Water dripping off branches and a gray mist hanging over everything. There was no sound but the patter of rain on his borrowed jacket and the lighter thuds where it hit the ground.

He squinted, but couldn't see Holly. He skirted the pond thinking she'd discovered the walking trail that led to his sister Marguerite's cottage. Maybe she was there right now having tea. Or more likely, knowing the way his family was treating her this weekend, Marguerite would have her out in the rain pulling weeds.

He walked on, the wet ground squelching beneath his feet.

Ahead, he saw a familiar shape. Lucky was lying down under the tree fort, chewing on a tennis ball. As he got closer he noticed it was a mostly bald tennis ball that he suspected Lucky had buried at some point and recently dug up.

She rose to her feet, soggy tail wagging hopefully, and dropped the ball at his feet where it made a tiny splash.

He picked it up, chucked it as far as he could and watched for a moment as the dog launched herself after it.

Clearly, he thought, looking up at the tree house, Holly was not at Marguerite's.

He stood for a moment in the rain, and then did something he hadn't done in more than a decade. He climbed a tree.

HOLLY WAS TAPPING AS FAST as she could into her iPad, her phone glued to her ear. She really had to get one of those earpiece things. Well, another one since she'd lost the last one.

She knew she was breaking the Prescott law about no cell phones outside of her one-hour-a-day allotment but, in the first place, Prescott wasn't home to be annoyed and in the second, when Rupert's wife called, she was not about to leave the woman waiting for a call back.

Not certain when Prescott would be getting back, she'd decided to find a discreet place outside to make her call. In the pouring rain there weren't too many options. The barns looked gross, the meditation yurt was probably not meant for cell phones. She didn't want to disturb Daphne's chi when the woman had been so nice to her.

She'd been blinking against the rain, Lucky crazed with excitement at her side, when she'd remembered the tree fort.

She took Lucky for a walk, not wanting to disappoint her biggest fan in the Chance household, and then threw the ball a few times. Then she felt she could sneak off into the tree house for a few stolen minutes with her smuggled phone.

Hoping Prescott was as good a builder as he was an architect, she'd climbed the rickety boards, as scared of breaking her electronics as she was afraid of breaking a bone, but the rungs held her. She pushed open the door and crawled into Prescott's first design.

She peeked down and Lucky gave one whine, then dropped to her belly and started chewing the ball.

The small space was dry which was pretty impressive. It smelled like old wood, and there was a faint odor of smoke that suggested the Chance kids hadn't only come here to read comic books.

There was enough light coming in the windows that she could see a stack of vinyl cushions on the floor that looked as though they'd come from old patio furniture. A couple of wine bottles with candles jammed in the top. One tattered paperback in a corner. A fantasy novel from ten years earlier.

She wasn't sure what she'd expected, but the interior of the tree house was cleaner and more impersonal than she'd thought. Somebody had cleaned it up at some point.

She shook out the vinyl lounge cushions, happy to see no signs of rodents, and pushed them into the corner and settled down to make her call.

She'd spoken to Iona Rupert once at a horrible fancy luncheon at Alistair's club when he'd made her run papers up for him to sign and he'd introduced her to his wife. Mrs. Rupert was Russian and gorgeous. Tall, blonde and shapely, with eyes the color of Bombay sapphire gin, she was clearly used to having her own way.

Rupert had introduced Holly to his wife as "my latest assistant," and the woman had given her a finger to shake and called her Halle.

She wasn't sure if it was an accent thing or if the woman actually didn't know her name. She wasn't about to correct her.

"Halle," she said, when Holly returned her call. "I have called you directly because I must have my house. My husband understands that this is very important. I hear you have not been able to convince Prescott Chance to build me a house." She sounded insulted at the notion that anyone would say no to her.

"We simply haven't found the correct location," she said, as soothing as she could. "He's very happy to design you a house, of course. I can tell you that he's excited at the opportunity, but he wants it to be exactly the right location. He's an artist, Mrs. Rupert. He has to feel the place."

"Yes that's all very well but I can't wait forever for the man to envision my house. Anyway, *I've* found the perfect location." Holly felt that the way she emphasized *I've* was her way of telling Holly that she wasn't doing her job properly. If the woman only knew that she'd taken to stalking the architect in hopes of convincing him to build anything so she could keep her job and pay off her loans.

Frankly she didn't care if he designed a square box, and she had a sneaking suspicion that so long as Mrs. Rupert could brag to her friends that she had a Prescott Chance-designed home, she wouldn't care if it was a square box either.

"Really?" Holly tried to sound enthusiastic.

"Yes. It's a stunning location overlooking the ocean at Malibu."

Holly had been keeping very close tabs on every inch of property that was for sale in California. "I haven't heard of that one."

"That's because it's not for sale. Not officially, but I know the wife. They're in financial trouble. For the right price, they'll sell. There's an existing house that will need to be torn town. A dreary old place from the twenties. When can you bring him to see it?"

Like he was a head waiter who could be summoned with a snap of the fingers.

"I'm not sure when he'd—"

"The owners are out of town for a week. I want him signed up before they return."

How the hell was she going to get Prescott to Malibu? "It's at least a five-hour drive, could we—"

"We'll fly, naturally. We'll take the Gulfstream. Tuesday works best for me."

"I'll do my best."

"I know you will, Halle." It sounded like a threat.

She was about to call Luis to vent and maybe ask advice, had her thumb on the send button, when she heard the scrape of the door opening. She shoved her phone under her as Prescott stuck his head through the boy-sized opening.

"Ah," he said, those intense eyes focusing on her. "I thought you might be in here."

CHAPTER 7

"Hi." She had no idea what else to say. She was ridiculously conscious of how small the space was, how intimate and that she had climbed up into the tree house he'd built without asking permission.

Not that she was certain there was an etiquette to entering an abandoned tree house.

To her surprise, Prescott didn't back out or invite her to climb down so he could discuss whatever it was he wanted her for. Instead, he climbed into the tree house with her, remarkably agile for a tall man. He wore a rain-speckled jacket much too grungy to be his. He shut the door behind him and, since he couldn't stand, crouched his way over to sit beside her on the vinyl cushions.

She could see a raindrop sparkling on his lashes. His hair was damp but otherwise he looked as perfectly crisp as always.

He glanced around. "I haven't been in here for probably fifteen years. Maybe more. Makes me feel like a kid again." He stretched out his long legs. "It stayed dry," he said, not without pride.

"Yes. It did."

There was silence but for the drumming of the rain on the roof. He was so still he made her fidgety. "How was the tux fitting?" she asked.

He turned to look at her and as their gazes connected she thought, not for the first time, how gorgeous he was. It wasn't only the sharply angled features, the high cheekbones and dark eyes that might or might not be native in origin. It was the energy he radiated. Not nervous energy, like hers, but a kind of quiet energy that drew her.

"It was a setup. They got me good, too. I didn't suspect a thing until I came out of the changing room in the ugliest powder blue tux you have ever seen." He grinned in self-mockery and she was happy to see he could laugh at himself. "They got pictures and everything."

He didn't seem too angry. More like he admired the way they'd managed the prank so successfully. She tried not to smile but it was impossible. "Pictures?" Oh, she really, really wanted to see those pictures.

"You knew." It wasn't a question, it was a statement.

She kept quiet because he was right.

He regarded her with the quiet intensity he brought to most things. "Why didn't you tell me? You're trying to suck up to me so I'll build a house for your boss. You could have told me."

She wrinkled her brow. In truth it hadn't even crossed her mind to tell him. She thought about how excited the boys had been—and they really were a bunch of boys when they got together, including Jack. "Because they trusted me. They let me in on the secret because they believed I wouldn't tell you." She couldn't stop her lips from twitching. "And it was funny seeing you get so upset about wearing an ugly rental tux."

He chuckled and his face was even more attractive when he laughed. "You should have seen it. Honest to God I thought Evan had lost his mind. If James hadn't made me feel like Cooper was such a poverty case we couldn't afford anything else I would have fallen in."

"So, you're not mad?"

"Naah. We went for lunch after, had a beer."

That probably explained things in Prescott speak.

"So, what are you doing up here?" he asked, turning all his energy to her once more.

"I needed a quiet place to think," she said, doing her best to look innocent.

"Thinking, huh?" He leaned closer and her heart began to do a strange fluttering dance in her chest.

She backed up but she was already against the wall. "It was, ah, hard to think with all the wedding preparation going on at the house."

"Thinking? That all you were doing?"

Her phone was barely tucked beneath her, she could feel the lump of it at her hip. Her iPad was on her lap. "I might have made some notes."

He pounced the way Lucky would pounce on her ball, only a lot more gracefully. She gave an involuntary start as he closed his hand immediately on her cell phone, so his hand grazed her hip. He lifted the phone and held it up.

Okay, so she was busted. She lifted her chin. "Fine. I needed to return a call. You weren't here. It couldn't bother you."

"But we had an agreement," he said, all low and sexy, not moving back so he was in her personal space and she could see the fine texture of his skin, smell the all-male scent of him.

She bit her bottom lip. "I know."

He seemed to find her mouth fascinating, so much so that she had to force herself not to nibble on her lip some more.

"Mrs. Rupert called," she admitted. "She is not the kind of person you don't call back."

"Mrs. Rupert?"

"Yes. She's found a site she thinks would be perfect." She rushed to speak before he could refuse. "It's not on the market so you can't say you've seen it because you haven't. But it's in Malibu."

"Malibu?"

"You promised me, Prescott. You promised five sites."

He seemed to consider her words. "But you promised me you'd only use your cell phone for one hour a day." He shook his head but there was a disturbing light in his eyes that in another man might be humor. "Seems to me there should be consequences."

"Consequences?" She hoped he wasn't thinking of throwing her out on her ear, though the way he was watching her mouth, and the gleam in his eyes that was moving from teasing to interested made her suspect kicking her out was not what he had in mind.

"I could simply keep you so busy you don't have time for cell phone hour."

They'd been fighting this moment since that first second when he'd walked out of his office to find her sitting on his car. She recalled the leap of recognition she'd felt, the strong attraction she'd felt to him physically even when he'd acted like an arrogant ass.

Her body had known, had always known that this was inevitable.

He reached and took a lock of her hair, twisting it

around his finger. She didn't pull away or move or do anything except start to melt.

Their gazes connected and she felt a fierce hunger deep in her belly. She tilted her face up even as he lowered to her mouth.

Oh, that first kiss. That stunning meeting of lips and his hands in her hair, and hers going to his shoulders, feeling the solid bulk, the warm muscles at play.

He pulled slowly away looking as stunned as she felt. He took a deep, shaky breath. "I don't do things like this."

"You don't?" He'd seemed fairly practiced to her. Plus, from her research that had somehow encompassed his private as well as his business life, she knew he was rarely without a woman in his life.

He shook his head impatiently. "Not like this. I'm an orderly man."

"Yes, you are."

He kissed her again, longer this time, deeper. "There is nothing orderly about you, about this."

Orderly would not be the first word that would come to her mind, either.

Her heart was racing, everything from her hair to her curling toes felt askew. Orderly? Not a chance.

"I choose carefully," he said, and then kissed her again as though he wanted to stop and couldn't. "But you, you make me feel reckless."

She smiled, feeling all her feminine power. "Good."

She kissed him back and as the rain drummed down outside, his hands began to move, tracing her shape, learning her with the same intense focus he'd bring to a piece of property on which he was considering designing a house.

And that thought acted like a thorough dunking in the Chance family pond.

She pulled back, banged her head on the plywood wall behind her, pushed him away to give herself a little breathing room.

"Wait, we shouldn't do this," she panted even as every cell in her body screamed yes, yes we should. "We work together."

He traced her from shoulder to hip, edging around her breast but not quite touching it in a way that made shivers dance down her body. "No. We don't work together. You work for someone who wants to hire me. So far, I haven't agreed."

"But you have to. And this—" She threw her hands up. "This will mess everything up."

"Why?"

"Because." She couldn't think of a lot of clear reasons because she couldn't really think, but in her gut she knew this was probably a bad idea. "Because the sex could be terrible and then things would be awkward."

Seriously? Had she actually just said that? She rewound her blabbermouth tape. Yep, she'd said that. One more reason why she shouldn't have sex with Prescott. He made her say really dumb things.

Fortunately, instead of being insulted he seemed amused. "Do you really think that's a possibility?"

"Yes." No! But her last boyfriend had seemed like he'd be studly. He was athletic, good looking, but between the sheets there'd been an excess of saliva and a lack of technique that had ruined things. She didn't feel like sharing that sad episode of her love life so she kept uncharacteristically silent while the rain tapped on the roof.

Prescott seemed like he was choosing words carefully,

then he said, "I don't want to boast, but I haven't heard any complaints."

"Like you would."

"What do you mean?"

She listed off a few critical items. "You're gorgeous, famous and rich. Not a lot of women are going to dump a guy like that for a lack of—" How to put this? "Chemistry in the bedroom."

Oh, lord. There went her mouth again running off without her. Challenge the guy's proficiency in bed. That was a good plan.

"Do you think you could be overthinking this?" His finger was still doing that hypnotic tracing movement and she did not think that lack of chemistry was going to be an issue.

"Yes. I overthink everything."

"Well, I don't want my first time with you to be in a tree house." He grinned in sudden memory. "Though my first time was in fact right here in this tree house."

Her mind raced ahead to the sleeping arrangements. "The bunk beds?"

"Please. Now that you've challenged my talent in the sack? You really think I'm going to have sex with you in a bunk bed under my parents' roof?"

"Probably not." And now that he was telling her it wasn't going to happen, she was more disappointed than relieved.

Then he teased her with a final, deep kiss. "When I take you to bed, it's going to be where I have lots of room and lots of time to make sure you get all the chemistry you can handle. Got it?"

She nodded, feeling every womanly part of her quiver at the thought.

HE'D NEVER WORKED to seduce a woman before. Not like this. Not even that first time in the tree house. Becca Brody had been her name. A year older than he was, a hell of a lot more experienced, she'd been the one doing the seducing. He'd gone into that tree house with her a boy and a few memorable hours later he'd emerged—well, a boy still but one who thought he was a man.

He and Becca had spent a lot of time in the tree house that summer he was sixteen. What she hadn't taught him they'd figured out together. From then until now, he'd never had a problem satisfying a woman.

And if they didn't seem interested or demanded a lot of wooing he rarely took the trouble. So why did this woman who always seemed to have her buttons done up wrong or mismatched socks have him plotting to send her to the moon and back?

Didn't make any sense.

And he didn't have time in his life for unnecessary complications.

Then she looked at him with her big green eyes and he remembered the feel of her impossible-to-tame hair in his hands, recalled the taste of her on his mouth, and he knew that one day very soon she'd be naked and in his bed.

The atmosphere in the bunk-bedded room was different the second night, with the tree house incident between them. He could hear her, restless beneath him. But then she did everything restlessly.

"Prescott?" she whispered.

"Yes?"

"Iona Rupert's ordered the Gulfstream and wants to fly

down Tuesday to see the site. She suggested you meet us at the airfield. We'll fly down together."

He could tell from Holly's tone that she hated passing on the message as much as he hated being ordered around by some woman married to a guy with too much money and no social conscience. Naturally, he wanted to refuse immediately. But he could hear the strain in her voice. She needed him to say yes so she could keep that wretched job. And because he found himself caring that she had enough money to scrimp by, he said, "I'll meet you at the site."

He heard her body roll and then she pushed her head over the side rail of her bunk bed as though they were kids at summer camp.

"Seriously? You'll do it?"

He leaned out and looked down at her. Sighed. "Holly, you make me bend my principles."

"You mean you'll design the Ruperts a house even if you don't love them or the site?"

"No." What did she take him for? "I meant my personal principles. I won't bend design principles." Some things were unshakable.

"Why don't you catch a ride with us?"

"I prefer not to be beholden."

"So, do you have your own private plane too?"

"No." It was true. He didn't own the entire plane. He shared it with another architect. He didn't like boasting about his wealth. It made him uncomfortable. The foolish part was he'd never gone into architecture to make a fortune. He'd found his calling. Most of his colleagues had predicted that his lack of sales technique and people skills would be his downfall. Strangely enough, he thought that those very qualities had added to his success, though he liked to think that he was hired because he was a very good architect.

By the time they left right after brunch Sunday morning, Prescott wondered if Daphne and Jack were planning to adopt Holly to round out the brood to an even dozen. They certainly treated her like one of the family. His mother said, as she was leaving, "And you won't forget to check on the napkins?"

"No. And I've got a friend who recently got married. I'll ask her about the candle holders I was telling you about. They'll be perfect for a fall wedding."

"I just hope we don't have to hold it under cover. It rains here as often as not."

"We'll figure it out," Holly said, as though she was somehow responsible for the wedding.

He wasn't at all surprised when Daphne enfolded Holly in a hug, or when Jack followed suit.

He was hugged in his turn and he vowed to himself not to leave it so long between visits.

HOLLY GLARED in her rearview mirror one more time. Why was Prescott stalking her in the stealth vehicle? She slowed so he could pass her and then he slowed, staying right behind her. Finally, irritated, she called his cell phone.

"Yes?" he answered.

"Why are you following me?"

"How did you get this number?"

"I asked you a question first."

He sighed. "I am following you because I don't trust that vehicle of yours will make it back to San Francisco."

Even though she had the same fears it was annoying to

have Mr. Rich Guy follow her like a stealth missile. "I have managed to drive thousands of miles in my life without your help, thank you."

"Okay. Now, how did you get my cell phone number? In fact, how did you find out about the phone?"

"Your mom mentioned calling you on it. So, I texted myself from your phone so I'd have the number."

"My phone was in my car all weekend." The unspoken message being as clear as if he'd shouted at her. Because I don't take my phone with me on a weekend at my parents' place. But, being Prescott, he didn't say the words, he let her divine them.

"I know. I used your magic key thing and let myself into your car and found the phone and then I called myself on it."

"You went to a lot of trouble to get my number." He sounded ridiculously smug, like she was a girl with a crush.

Her body went hot at the memories of their time alone together in the tree house.

Damn it, he had good reason to be smug. She was a girl with a crush. A huge, problematic crush on a very rich, very sexy architect who usually dated women who were also rich, sophisticated, and, if her research was to be believed, sometimes titled.

"You are so hard to get hold of, I figured I should at least have your cell number." And she had been pleased to discover he was human enough to own a cell even if he never used it.

"Well, you called and I answered, so I guess it worked."

"You're not overtaking me," she said, watching that amazing car plod along behind her, keeping pace.

"No. I'm not."

"Fine," she snapped, and disconnected.

He followed her all the way home and then, just when she began to think he had ideas about trying to have sex with her in her tiny shared apartment, he waved and carried on his way.

Okay, fine, so he wasn't in a rush to have sex with her. He'd probably only been teasing anyway.

Which was good. Excellent. She couldn't imagine a worse idea than getting involved with a man who pretty much held her career in the palm of his genius-architect-who-never-compromises hand.

olly had dreaded flying with Iona Rupert. Even on a short flight, she couldn't imagine what they'd talk about. But, as it turned out, she needn't have worried. Holly pulled into the parking lot in front of the private airport, parked and got out. Iona's limo pulled up just as she was approaching the door.

The chauffeur jumped out and opened the back and Iona got out of it, followed by a dapper young man who turned out to be her personal assistant. A second man emerged from the limo. He quietly introduced himself as Lionel Wethers, Mrs. Rupert's lawyer.

Iona hadn't been too pleased that Prescott was meeting them at the site. Holly had thought she deserved a tiny word of praise for getting him there at all, but it seemed like Iona thought she'd screwed up by not getting him on board the Gulfstream.

They never even sat in the fancy lounge at the airport. The second Iona entered, a gorgeous young guy in a dark suit came forward. "Mrs. Rupert," he said. "Wonderful to see you again."

"Thank you, Carl."

"Everything's ready. Let's get you on board."

Carl turned out to be the flight attendant, though he was more like a maître d'. Holly couldn't shake a sneaking suspicion that Mr. Rupert's plane crew was also gorgeous but female.

Carl led Iona to the plane, describing the weather ahead as "glorious." Her assistant and her lawyer followed Iona, like two lap dogs, leaving Holly to bring up the rear.

When she entered the plane she had a real rich girl/poor girl moment. Did people seriously live like this? The plane was divided into two sections. Up front was a luxurious seating area, with a meeting table that would also double as a dining table. Beside it were a leather sofa and a couple of chairs.

A small screen separated the front from the back where a bed took up one side and a couple of leather recliners occupied the other side.

Iona settled herself on the couch and her two henchmen took their places, one at her side and the other in one of the club chairs. Holly hesitated, not sure whether to take the other club chair or sit beside Iona.

While she was trying to decide, Iona glanced at her coldly. "We'll be having a meeting, here, Halle. You can sit in the back."

As she made her way to the other side of the screen she realized that even on a private jet, she still got to sit in coach.

Luckily, her sense of humor kicked in and she spent a happy hour trying all the settings on the chair and sipping a cappuccino served to her in a china cup with a fancy R logo on it. She suspected the coffee was as good as anything you'd get in Rome.

When they arrived at the private airfield, a limo was

waiting for them, it's engine running so that they were whisked from plane to limo and onward to their destination with not so much as a second of waiting around.

A short drive brought them to the property.

Even though she was beginning to despise Iona Rupert, it was tough to argue with the woman's taste in real estate.

The location was spectacular, an acreage on the Malibu beach front.

As the limo drove through the gates and pulled up in the drive, Holly noted a rental Prius already there. Prescott stepped out.

She'd been trying not to think about him or about the steamy kissing session in the tree house, but she'd been as successful as she'd been when she'd tried to take up meditation. Monkey mind, they called it when your thoughts went all over the place and refused to focus. Well, her monkey mind kept swinging from branch to branch, away from what she wanted to concentrate on and focusing instead on Prescott Chance.

He sent her a quick nod, and their gazes connected only for an instant, but that was all it took to remind her that she was seriously fluttery when he was around. He'd promised her sex, well, he'd more threatened her with it, if the promise of satisfaction could ever be a threat, and from Sunday night until now she'd thought of little else.

Would she let him take her to bed? She wasn't even sure he'd meant it, had suspected he might be teasing her, and then their gazes connected and all she could think about was getting him alone.

Then Iona Rupert stepped forward and her mind was dragged right back to the here and now. "Prescott Chance," Iona cried, as she went toward him with outstretched arms. No handshake for Prescott, he got the European, two-cheek kissing greeting, which he accepted with the same smooth calmness he did everything.

"My husband and I are so delighted you are going to design us a house," she said, linking her arm into his. She leaned her spectacular body against him and glanced up sideways through her ice blue cat's eyes.

When Iona turned on the full force of her charm and sexuality, Holly had no trouble understanding how Rupert had fallen for her. Prescott, she suspected, was more immune, though looking at him now you wouldn't know it. He let her lean on him, let her pet him. She introduced him to her lackeys then waved a hand in Holly's direction. "And of course you know Halle."

"Holly," he said, extricating himself from Iona and striding forward and holding out his arms in the exact imitation of how Iona had greeted him. To Holly's shock he leaned forward and kissed both cheeks, pausing to whisper in her ear, "What a bitch."

She tried not to laugh, or to go too weak at the knees. The trouble with him getting so close was that it reminded her of how he felt in her arms, how much she'd responded to his kisses and the fact that she had no idea if he seriously planned to pursue her.

And what she'd do if he did.

He turned away from her then and Iona was smart enough to include Holly more definitely into the group that proceeded up the path to view the property.

She was happy that he'd chosen to make a big deal of her in front of Iona, but that bitch comment, while totally justified, made her worry about how eager he'd be to design a house for Iona, especially when she'd pretty much bullied him into coming out today.

Nothing of his distaste for the woman showed on his face. He listened while she talked. Nodded a few times.

They came to a vista and she caught her breath. She'd rarely seen anything so beautiful as the view from this private estate.

Iona barely glanced at it. All her attention was on Prescott. Her lawyer and her assistant were both focused on her. Holly was focused on Prescott, trying to gauge his reaction and to decide if there was anything she could do to influence him positively. He glanced around, as though taking in the grandeur of the view and the complete isolation of the property, but with Prescott it was impossible to tell.

"There's this annoying outcrop here that partially obscures the view from the lower floors. Can you fix it?"

"I never fix anything," he said.

Iona stared at her expensive architect as though he'd slapped her. She was clearly a woman unused to people speaking to her that way. Holly instinctively hastened to intervene.

"What Prescott means," she said soothingly, "is that the way he designs, he incorporates the features of a property. He works with the natural surroundings rather than trying to tame nature to his vision." She was paraphrasing some of what she'd read on the company website, splicing in what she'd read about him and, of course, she knew him well enough now that she could fill in a lot of his unspoken words.

She felt like a translator at the UN after that. Iona would say something, Prescott would give her a short, cryptic answer, and Holly would either put what he'd said into terms a polite person would use or make something up that sounded good.

As he walked to various bits of the property and stood there, Iona followed, her ice pick heels tapping along the flagstone paths. "My husband and I were at a dinner in a home you designed in Sydney, Australia. I was thinking that this lot is very similar to that one."

"I never repeat myself."

Iona glanced at Holly, her eyes snapping.

"What Prescott means," she said, wishing Prescott would be a tiny bit less cryptic with the woman who could have her fired with a snap her perfectly manicured fingers, "is that he respects that you wouldn't want to live in a house knowing there was an identical one somewhere else in the world. He would design something unique, both for you and for the site."

Prescott sent her a glance that suggested he was enjoying hearing her turn his vinegar into honey. She was glad somebody here was having a good time.

She pushed her mass of hair off her neck where the sun was making her feel prickly.

He was clearly irritated with this posse following him but for some reason didn't shoo them away. Holly decided to do it for him before he completely alienated Mrs. Rupert. She said, "Prescott always likes to spend a few minutes in solitude to really get the feel of the land. If it doesn't speak to him, he can't build on it. Perhaps we should—"

"Yes, of course," Iona interrupted her. "Take your time, Prescott. We'll sit in the gazebo."

Instead of being furious at the way he'd brushed her off, Iona seemed to want his services even more. "He's such an artist," she announced as they walked to the gazebo, a pretty structure that looked like it came from *The Sound of Music*. As they entered the glassed-in structure hidden away under the trees, she said, "Of course, this kitschy thing will have to go."

With Prescott out of hearing, Holly was once more ignored while Iona told her lawyer to get the architect under contract. "I want to celebrate my husband's sixty-fifth birthday party in our new home," she said.

"Sixty-five?" Holly blurted, "But that's—"

"Next year. Exactly." She widened her eyes dramatically, "Everyone will be there. I shall unveil my house at this party. I've already hired the most famous pianist in the world to play for us, I've booked movie stars for the day. I cannot have delays."

Holly stared out the window, looking at Prescott, who'd wandered a bit and was now sitting on that very outcropping of rock that Iona had wanted blasted out of her view corridor. She wasn't sure if he was meditating, invoking his probably nonexistent Cherokee ancestors or daydreaming. As usual, he was still. So still he could have been one of those granite stone features Iona wanted to blow to pieces.

At last, he rose, turned and walked toward them.

Please, please, please. She whispered silently.

Before he got to the gazebo, Iona jumped to her feet and rushed out to meet him. The rest of them followed her out.

"Well?" she said, before Prescott could open his mouth. "Wasn't I clever? Isn't it the most perfect spot?"

"It's a beautiful piece of paradise," he agreed.

"And can you start right away? I must have the house ready for my husband's birthday party next year."

"Mrs. Rupert—"

"Iona, please."

"Iona. If I don't feel the design when I sit with the land, then I don't take the commission."

Her caressing tone turned suddenly sharp. "But you must have felt something?"

"I appreciated the natural beauty, of course. But for me, personally, there's no challenge here. If I can't feel the design organically, I can't create it." Then he nodded, said, "Good day to you." And walked away.

Iona stood there for half a minute and then turned to Holly, her eyes cold with outrage. "You've got one week to change his mind or get me a site he'll design on. One week."

She stomped back to the limo, and Holly trailed behind wondering how any of this was her fault, but knowing somehow that the Ruperts would find a way to blame her.

When they got back to the cars, Prescott was standing there. Iona rushed forward. "You changed your mind."

He looked at her coldly. "I never change my mind."

She looked in danger of throwing a monumental hissy fit, but controlled herself with an effort, the ice blue eyes flashing in a way that suggested Holly was going to get all the pent-up fury she couldn't unleash on Prescott.

"Holly," he said. "You should ride back with me."

Iona's eyes flashed once more, but then she turned her fake sweet smile on Holly. "What a wonderful idea. She's such a lovely girl. Perhaps you two can work something out." She walked up to Prescott. "I do so want you to design my new house." She stroked his arm. "I'd be very grateful."

He smiled at her and did the European cheek kiss thing again and then shook hands with the two men. He opened the passenger side door for Holly and, feeling like she was a delivery package being handed off, she climbed in.

She waited until Prescott was inside and both doors were closed. Iona was being tenderly handed into the limo.

"Really?" she cried. "Really? You had to piss off the

scariest woman in the world who also happens to be my boss's wife?"

He looked at her as though he had no idea what she was talking about. "I came down here, took an entire morning out of my schedule, to see this property."

"And then did nothing but insult Iona Rupert. Why? Why would you do that?"

"Because you asked me to." He said it so simply and she realized that for Prescott this was a really big deal. He'd gone out of his way. For her.

Okay, he'd also gone all Prescott the Shaman on her, but in his way he'd really put himself out.

"Oh, well. Thanks."

"You're welcome."

"So, how could you not be in love with that site? It was amazing. Is it because Iona is so annoying that you don't want to design a house there?"

"No."

She shifted to look at his face more clearly. "Then why?"

"It's difficult to explain. I can imagine all kinds of buildings on that property but none of them would be mine. It's kind of impossible to articulate."

"Need to get the go-ahead from your Cherokee ancestors?" she asked. She was half joking, but only half.

"Kumeyaay," he said.

"What?"

"Kumeyaay. Those would have been the native people most likely living in this area."

"Oh. And do they talk to you?"

"No. No one talks to me. It's a kind of vision thing that I can't explain. It happens or it doesn't."

"Like love," she said, suddenly understanding.

"Love?" He sounded like she was now speaking in Kumeyaay.

"Yes. You can meet somebody who is absolutely perfect for you and all your friends think he's amazing, but you just don't feel it. And then the most unlikely person walks into your life and bam, there it is."

She hadn't started out thinking of the two of them, but when she said the words she thought that Prescott was the last man in the world who should make her knees weak and her girl parts hum, and yet he did.

She gazed out the window as her best chance of quick promotion in Rupert's company faded. At least she could thank Prescott for not making her ride home with a pissed-off Iona.

Wait a minute; Iona had a private jet. How were she and Prescott getting home? Since she didn't feel like asking Prescott, knowing he wouldn't have offered her a ride if he couldn't get her home, she sat back and relaxed.

There was something so restful about Prescott. He never felt the urge to fill a silence for the sake of filling it, he didn't fidget or fuss or ever do more than one thing at once. He made the incessant buzz that was always vibrating under her skin quiet a little.

When they pulled into another private airfield and she saw a smaller version of the same Gulfstream she'd flown down on, she wasn't even surprised. Except for one thing. "You said you didn't have a private plane." She was shocked that a man of such integrity would tell a lie.

"I don't. I share it with another architect."

She grabbed her case and got out of the car. "You are such a head case."

The interior of this plane was a lot less fancy and much more business oriented than her last ride.

The pilot wasn't in uniform, simply nodded when Prescott told him she'd be riding along, and told them to climb on board.

They did. When she entered the plane, she struck a pose that she hoped mimicked Iona and put on a cartoon-character Russian accent. "Where is my personal butler? Who will bring me my cappuccino in my personalized bone china cup?"

He shook his head at her. "I think there's some bottled water in the fridge if you want it."

"So much more than I want to sit in the back of the plane like a piece of luggage."

"She didn't seriously do that to you?"

"Oh, she did."

"I don't know how you can work for those people."

He passed her a bottle of water, took one for himself, and they settled across from each other in lounge type chairs that were nowhere near as fancy as those on the Ruperts' plane, but she was much happier to be here. "I won't be working for them much longer if we can't find you a property to fall in love with."

She unscrewed the cap and sucked back some cold water, feeling as though she were washing the bad taste of the morning out of her mouth.

"I don't need to love it. I need to respect it, understand it. See it."

She settled back in her seat. "Can you? If you really don't like someone, will you design them a house? Or do your personal feelings for the client get in the way?"

He considered her question. "Obviously, I'd rather work for clients I at least respect, but no. If the site speaks to me, it speaks to me. My work will be around a lot longer than the Ruperts."

And there was that blissfully unconcerned arrogance that tickled her every time. Because, of course, that was true. Long after they were all dead, Prescott's homes would still probably be lived in and valued.

"I suppose you couldn't give me any hints on what really moves you? I've only got two more chances to wow you."

He pulled his water bottle away from his mouth. "Two? We agreed on five locations. You've got one left."

Her mouth dropped open. "You can't count today. That wasn't my idea, that was Iona's."

He shrugged. "I've got other clients. I can't waste any more time on this. One more. That was our deal."

"One more," she wailed. "I can't stand the pressure."

He looked at her with a very disturbing twinkle in his eyes. "I might be able to give you a pretty broad hint of what I like."

"Really? How?"

"I could show you my apartment. I designed it to suit me." His gaze rested on her and she felt the pull, the attraction that was turning into a need.

She took another sip of water, feeling the cool liquid slide down her throat. Somehow she did not think he was taking her to his apartment to help her find a building site that would speak to his inner vision. Their gazes connected. "Is this along the lines of showing me your etchings?"

He grinned at her. "Something like that. I believe we have a date."

"A date?" She tilted her head. Regarded him. So perfectly groomed. The breeze had tossed her curls all over the place, but he looked as though he'd stepped off the front cover of *GQ*. Not even a speck of sand or dust had dared cling to his shoes. "A date is usually an invitation to dinner, maybe a movie. All you're asking for is sex."

His brows rose infinitesimally. "Would you like to go out to dinner?"

"Yes."

"All right."

He was impossible. Impossibly everything. Sexy, cool, successful. Imperturbable. She couldn't imagine sitting all through dinner with him, trying to make small talk when they both knew how the evening would end. She couldn't imagine she'd even be able to taste her food. "But I'd like to see your apartment first."

CHAPTER 9

*H*e might not have grinned in delight but the slight movement of his facial muscles told her he was pleased.

She spent the rest of the flight wondering what she'd done and feeling thankful that she'd slipped into her best lingerie this morning.

Fortunately, Prescott kept his plane in a different private air field than the Ruperts kept theirs. Again, it wasn't so over the top with the private limos and door-to-door valet service, not that there was anything shabby about walking off a private jet, heading for a secured parking area and jumping into a Tesla. Not too shabby at all, she thought as she settled herself into the passenger seat. Her cell phone buzzed like a hornet stuck in her pants. She looked at call display surreptitiously and was not surprised to see Iona's number flash.

Well, the hell with it. She didn't have a one-hour-a-day deal with Prescott right now, and besides he'd plunged her career back into serious jeopardy.

She clicked through to the call. Before she'd identified

herself Iona was issuing orders in a crisp, cold tone. "Halle, I will have my house."

She said it as though Holly were personally standing in her way instead of killing herself to get the woman the architect of her dreams. For a second she contemplated informing Iona that she was planning to sleep with the architect in question, as though she were sacrificing herself in order for the Ruperts to get their house. But really she knew that would be boasting. She hadn't missed the carnal way Iona had been checking Prescott out, as though he were a particularly delectable Beluga caviar.

"I'm doing everything I can," she assured the woman.

"What did he say about the site? Did he give you any reasons?"

"Only the same ones he gave you earlier. It doesn't speak to him. He's an artist. That's how he works."

"Well, he'll be a much richer artist if he gives me what I want. And it will be in your best interests too. I have a great deal of influence with my husband. I can help your career, you know." She didn't bother voicing the equally powerful truth. That she could end her career with Rupert as easily.

"I'll keep that in mind."

Iona was gone before she'd finished speaking.

Prescott said, "Iona?"

"Yes. That woman is going to make my life hell if I don't give her what she wants."

To her surprise, he took her hand. "Come on. Let's turn the Ruperts off for a few hours."

A thrill went through her from where their hands touched all the way to her toes. There was something about Prescott that made her feel reckless and sexy.

All her research, and she'd done quite a bit, had failed to hint at where Prescott actually lived. His address was always given as the building where his office was located. There were no quotes about his ranch or his oceanfront mansion or the house he'd designed himself in the Sierra Nevada foothills. All inquiries led to the blank wall of Prescott's mania for privacy and, like so much else about him, became part of his mystique and his mythology.

When he pulled into the parking garage for a brick building in downtown San Francisco, she almost wasn't surprised. An urban apartment was the last thing she'd have imagined and the perfect place for him to live. They stepped from his car to an elevator that whooshed them up, past the lobby, all the way to his penthouse.

The elevator opened and she was in a lobby foyer. The door ahead of her looked like a normal door. Then he opened it and ushered her inside.

She stepped in and gaped. "Oh, my," she said, turning in a slow circle.

His penthouse extended over two floors. He'd had part of the upper floor removed so that a huge open space was the central feature of the apartment. It was lean, industrial chic. Utterly stunning. Then she turned to glance out of the large windows and sucked in a breath at the view.

A few pieces of art hung on the walls and she knew without being told that they were originals, some by artists she even recognized.

"Is that a real Jose Bernal?" she asked, stepping forward for a closer look.

"You know art?" He seemed surprised. As well he should.

"Rupert has one in his office."

Her shoes clicked against the polished wood flooring. She didn't even know where to put down her bag. The place was like a gallery. "Do you actually live here?"

"Of course I do."

"But..." She thought about the apartment she and Luis shared, the half-read books on most of the surfaces, magazines, sections of newspaper, the sports equipment leaning against the walls, the DVDs from where Luis was halfway through *Game of Thrones*. The bits of clothing and junk that collected all over the place. "Where's your stuff?"

"I put my stuff away, like most adults."

She shook her head. "I would need staff following me around and cleaning up after me to ever have a place this neat. Wow."

"Come on, I'll show you upstairs."

He led her up a staircase that appeared to be suspended in the air, to the upper floor. There were three bedrooms up there, he told her. "The guest room, which mostly I keep for my mother and sisters. They like to come down sometimes and shop. And my studio," he opened a door into a light-filled room that contained a large desk with a computer monitor bigger than their TV at home, a drafting table, and one small filing cabinet.

Everything was put away. She had not the whisper of a hint what he was working on.

"You're frowning, what?"

"I don't think it's healthy to be this neat," she told him.

He took her hand once more. It was so different to have him showing her physical affection that she was pulled along by more than his hand in hers.

Along the hall, he opened the final door and her stomach did a little flip. Since she'd seen everything else, this must be his bedroom.

And it was. He held the door open for her to enter first.

"Oh, my," she said. He might be a Zen-like minimalist everywhere else, but a hint of his sensual nature flowed in his bedroom. The king-sized bed made her muscles relax just looking at it. The bedding was black and gray with hints of icy blue, silk and cotton and wool, she could almost feel the different textures from looking at them.

The art on these walls was much more personal. A female nude reclined above the bed. She stopped. Stared. "Oh, my God, Is that—"

"A Picasso. Yes." He stood beside her to look at the painting. "A minor work, obviously. I have very little need for wealth, but I do enjoy being able to buy great art."

The other art on the walls wasn't something you'd expect to see hanging in the D'Orsay in Paris, but she suspected the names on the canvases would one day be household names.

"The bathroom's through there," he said.

Because she had to see it, and besides she was feeling suddenly shy, she walked to the open doorway and sighed. The tub alone made her want to move in here and never leave. The bathroom was bigger than her bedroom and featured a deep soaker tub with room for at least two people in some kind of stone that you'd find in an upper-end spa. The stand-alone steam shower made her sigh with envy.

A huge picture window was frosted but the upper half offered a stunning view of the city.

He looked at her and then smiled.

"What?"

"In my home, you're like that unexpected splash of color on a canvas. The element that doesn't fit and yet somehow brings the whole together."

She was so touched by the compliment that she defaulted to sarcasm. "You mean like a pair of dirty socks on a perfectly clean floor?"

He laughed. "A very nice, colorful pair of socks."

And then he stepped closer, put a hand to the back of her head and kissed her.

She melted. Simply melted. All the stress and strain of dealing with Iona dropped away like sheets of ice in the hot sun. His body just brushed hers and she felt the power of the chemistry between them, the pull-pull of two bodies drawn inevitably together.

The kissing in the tree house, the awareness they'd tried to ignore in the bunk beds, all that had been extended fore-play for this moment. Finally, they had space and privacy and time.

She shut her mind to the million things she had to do, to the unreasonable demands of not one but two Ruperts, and gave herself over to this moment, and this man.

She'd be up half the night anyway, in a final last-ditch effort to find a property for Prescott, now that Iona had added to her stress by giving her only a week. Plus, she need to make certain Rupert's team had all the information they needed before Rupert flew to Tokyo with an acquisition team to buy up an ailing tech company two days from now.

To take a few hours for herself seemed like an act of sanity in an insane world.

So, she let herself go, melted into his arms, let herself enjoy the powerful attraction.

He teased her mouth gently, ran his hands over her body with the ease of practice, the ease of a man who knew and enjoyed women.

She did some exploring of her own, running her hands up his back, over a cashmere sweater so fine it felt like stroking a cloud.

Not that she wouldn't have been happy to make love in that spa bathroom, but she wasn't sorry when he took her hand and led her into the bedroom. He kissed her, more deeply, and she felt the answering quiver deep inside her body as she opened her mouth to him and felt every other part of her prepare to open.

He teased, dallied, and slowly, oh, so slowly, began to undress her.

And then Prescott, a man who never rushed, who put time and focus into everything, lost it. He muttered guttural, earthy words as he began to rip the remaining clothes off her body. He was like a wild thing that had been leashed too long and suddenly found freedom. His hands were everywhere, his mouth kissed and nuzzled and nipped. Those eyes that usually operated on full focus were wild, barely focused at all.

She felt him losing control and nothing in all her life had ever excited her more. She loved this power. *This is what I do to him.*

And naturally, the more she felt her own power the more she gave it away. As his need grew, so did her own. They pulled at clothing, tossing things to the floor, and when he flipped back the lovely, heavy comforter and pushed her to the bed, she grabbed at him as she went down, pulling him with her.

They rolled, each digging deeper, trying to get to the core of the other. She wanted everything. She wanted to taste him, smell him, take his very essence into her. She felt him doing the same, as though he could absorb her into his bloodstream.

Her skin was so sensitive that when he nuzzled her neck she felt a throb down deep inside her and when his lips moved down to her nipple, sucking one into his mouth, she heard a cry she only vaguely recognized as her own, so sweet was the pull, so intense the echoing pull in her core.

His skin was smooth, like hot silk. No, smoother than

silk, like warm, smooth skin, not like something that could be compared to anything else. She licked at him, needing to taste him, inhaled the scent of him, wanting to own that scent, to forever recognize it. She felt that if she suddenly went blind she'd always know him, so intimately did she learn his body with all of her senses.

They touched, teased, excited each other and then he slipped a hand between their bodies and began to play with her most intimate places, driving her up, up, until the wave took her and she crested, crying out, arching beneath him, her body bowing before collapsing, spent and soft. But not nearly satisfied. He reached over and dealt with a condom, not so elegantly as she'd imagined. She could feel his haste in the way he fumbled the thing on, which only made her want him more.

Then she was opening for him. In the light of day, there was nowhere to hide. The bedroom was lit so when she stared into his eyes she saw everything. Her heart began to pound and as he entered her, she felt as though her entire body, her mind, every piece of her cried, *Yes!*

Then the pounding need took them. His eyes grew even darker, if that was possible, and she felt drawn into his mystery, happy to follow, needing to follow. As his movements became more frenzied, a drop of sweat fell on her shoulder. His skin was slick, as was hers, she was thrusting up, meeting him, hearing the slap of skin on skin, the inner slide as their bodies danced, and then she felt the build toward the crest. The sweet ache as her body drove her up and suddenly they were on top of the world. Their gazes connected. She could barely see him, her vision was so passion blurred, and then with a huge cry, she felt her body contract, every inch of her trembling. As she milked him, he drove in and in again until his cry echoed hers.

He slumped on top of her, heavy and ungainly, hot and spent.

She smiled and kissed his shoulder. She could see a pulse pounding.

Yes, she thought. Yes.

For a long time they lay entwined together, getting their breath back, blissed out. She smiled into his hair. "If your body could talk right now, what would it say?"

He raised his head. His eyes were still heavy-lidded and sexy. "Thank you."

She smiled, feeling ridiculously full of herself. "Mine is saying, 'Yes.'"

He seemed to contemplate her words. Nodded. "That too." Then he collapsed once more.

CHAPTER 10

"I've got one chance left. One," she told Luis over the weak coffee she'd brewed, using the last of the coffee in the apartment. "One! And a week to find it."

"Can't believe that bitch stole your number four. That's not right."

"I know. But Prescott's completely inflexible on some things. Drives me nuts." She, who could change direction on a whim. She pushed her hands through her hair. Part of her lack of focus was simple exhaustion. She'd snatched maybe an hour of sleep in the midst of getting everything ready for the Tokyo meetings. Then, before his plane took off, Rupert had texted her a list of instructions. He wasn't coming straight home. He was heading to London and wanted her to set up meetings there. Iona had discovered a young fashion designer she predicted was going to be big and wanted to own the label.

"Seriously, he thinks he can buy people," she wailed to Luis. "It's my day off and now I have to buy him a designer. And I have to find Prescott a property. And we're out of coffee."

"Come on, walk with me. I need to see my abuela. I promised I'd help pack some boxes for them. She'll feed us for sure. And the coffee pot is always on."

"Are they moving already?"

"Sure. They bought a place in Mexico. Near family."

"Did they sell their house?"

"No. But it will go fast. Maybe not for as much as they'd hoped because of the weird lot, but they'll still walk away with a nice retirement nest egg."

They walked to his grandparents' house. Her internal body clock was set to Tokyo time. Her eyes were blurry from looking at real estate listings, both whisper and real. She'd expanded her search in every direction she could think of. All she needed was something, anything, Prescott Chance would say yes to.

The house of Luis's grandparents had been built by his great-great somebody or other and she wasn't entirely certain that there'd been much of a building code back then. She'd always loved its quirky lines, but she could see it would be a tough sell, she who pretty much had an advanced degree in real estate thanks to the past few weeks.

A volley of Spanish greeted Luis when his grandmother opened the door in her usual uniform of black skirt, white blouse, black cardigan and the gold cross that always hung from her neck. It wasn't the usual babble. Holly might only understand one in five words, but she could hear the undertone of worry. Finally, the woman wore down and pulled Holly in for a hug. "Holly, so nice to see you. Come in, join us for *cafecito con pan dulce*." Heaven. Luis had been right. The coffee was fresh and the little sweets from the local bakery were exactly what her exhausted mind and body needed.

"Gracias," she said. "But I'm not sure I should." She

glanced at Luis, knowing he'd be honest with her on whether her presence was a good or a bad thing for his grandmother, but he nodded.

Rapidly, Luis translated what was going on. "The real estate agent had bad news for them. The way the house was built, it never complied with any guidelines. So, if you pull the place down, you have to build much smaller. So, basically, they're screwed."

"But this is right in the heart of The Mission." The home might not be anyone's dream house, but with the right vision— She nearly choked on her coffee.

Luis stared at her. "What?"

"Challenge. Urban density. Small footprint. Prescott's always talking about those things but he's never done one."

Luis looked at her like she might be out of her mind. "Prescott Chance? Are we talking about the world-famous architect who has said no to properties you and I could only dream about?"

She nodded, her curls smacking her face in her enthusiasm. "See? That's the thing. Those are the properties everybody shows him because that's what he's done before, that's what the super rich will pay for. But he doesn't care about that. He designs for his own reasons, a bunch of which I don't even understand, but he's very interested in better urban design." A beat of excitement drummed in her belly. "I think this could be it."

"Chica, you've only got one card left to play. You sure this is the right one?"

"No. Frankly, I'm not sure of anything right now, including what day it is. All I know is that I've trolled properties from all over the world and all I could picture was Prescott giving that cold shrug and saying it didn't speak to him." She gave her own shrug. "This is crazy and completely out of the box, but I think this one might just speak to him. Whatever happens, I'll have done everything I could to find the Ruperts a property. And I will never have to look at another real estate listing as long as I live."

"And neither will I," he said in relief. It was true, she'd forced him to look at more properties in the past few days than any person should have to. She'd said, "You know, one day you could buy something like this if your startup takes off." And he'd replied that no matter how rich he got he'd never want an estate that big.

She wondered if Prescott was suffering a similar fatigue from designing only the highest of high end. Maybe he'd like to try something a little more real. And if you wanted a design challenge, this was your spot.

"I need to call him."

"You're sleep deprived and desperate. I want you to be sure."

She wasn't sure about anything, but there was a tingling in her belly and she decided to follow its promptings. Yes, it might lead to disaster, but most roads seemed to lead there anyway as far as she and the Ruperts were concerned.

"I'm calling him."

Naturally, she couldn't get straight through to Prescott. Not even sharing orgasms with the man gave her that access mostly because nobody had access. She called his cell and a computerized voice told her the cell phone customer was not available. She called his office and left an urgent message with the receptionist who said she'd get the message to him the second he was available. Like when he was finished communing with the spirits of his ancestors or working on a design or some combination of both. Whatever he actually did tucked up high in that scarily quiet office.

It was only ten minutes later when he called her, which she suspected had a lot to do with their recent extracurricular activities.

"Hi," he said, warm and sexy and un-Prescott like.

She felt herself blushing and with a gesture to Luis and his grandmother walked out the front door and sat on the stoop. "Hi, yourself."

"I was thinking about you this morning," he said. "I never get distracted, but you are distracting me."

She couldn't imagine a greater compliment, though she suspected he didn't see it that way.

"That's good."

"You calling to let me know you want to try it again tonight?"

"Well, yes, now you mention it, I do. But I called because I have another site for you to see."

He groaned. "No more planes. If I can't drive there in an hour, I'm saying no right now."

"You can walk to it," she said. "In fact, you should come over right now. I'm here." She gave him the address.

"That's in The Mission," he said.

"Yes, it is. You want challenge? You want a small urban footprint? You want to put your money where your sustainable future mouth is? This is your place."

"I've never heard you sound so confident about a place before."

She was pulling on every bit of self-confidence she had left after almost eight months with Rupert. "I've never felt so confident."

"This is your last site. We're clear on that, right?"

"Yep."

There was a pause. "I could use some air."

She jumped up on the cement stoop and pushed her fist in the air. "Okay, I'll be here."

Fortunately, Luis's grandmother had never heard of Prescott Chance so she didn't get unrealistic hopes since she didn't have any hopes at all regarding a friend of Holly's walking over to look at her home. She was more worried about transporting her household saints and her *veladoras*, her collection of religious candles, without anything getting broken.

She packed the saints herself, saying a prayer over each, while Luis hefted furniture that they'd targeted for Goodwill.

While Holly wrapped good china, she wondered what she'd done? In that rush of excitement she'd gotten carried away. As usual. If she ever sat down and thought things through she wouldn't get herself in these messes, like ever making this foolish deal with Prescott in the first place.

But then if she hadn't met him, hadn't dared him to push her away, hadn't challenged him into accepting her ridiculous proposal, then she wouldn't have enjoyed some of the best sex of her life.

He made her feel things she had no business feeling for a man who lived in a different stratosphere from her in so many ways. They couldn't be more different. He was rich and she was in student loan debt; he was sleek, sure of himself, self contained, and she was a wild mess of insecurities and dreams. If he got his inspiration from the earth, she thought she must get hers from the wind. It blew in, picked her up and carried her along a little way then usually dumped her on her butt.

Impulsive. That was her problem. Whether she was daring a world-famous architect to design her boss a house or getting naked with same architect without thinking through the consequences at all. Consequences, she thought, pushing a hand through her tangle of curls. Now that she'd slept with him things would always be different.

By the time he knocked on the door she'd bounced from euphoria to terror and back again so many times she was dizzy. Luis had taken her off the good china, clearly afraid she'd smash it all. Instead, she was assigned to matching plastic food containers with their lids, packing the matched sets and tossing those that didn't have a lid.

She put everything down when she heard the knock. Forced herself to draw in a full breath and walked to the front door. She opened it and Prescott was standing there.

When he gazed at her she forgot that she was supposed to show him the property and sell him on all the excellent reasons why he should consider designing a house here. All she could think of was how much she wanted him again. Her body pulsed with need, a drumbeat that seemed to bang inside her veins. Want him want him want him need him want him need him.

His eyes softened when he continued to regard her and she felt as though he was reading her mind, or picking up the beat of her desire for him. Powerful. It was too powerful.

Desire was fine, but she couldn't let it become need. That would be a bad idea on every level.

"Hi," he said at last and she felt as though they'd been standing there staring at each other for a long time.

"Hi." She didn't want to blush. That was foolish, adolescent, too much like a girl with a crush. But even as she tried to keep the color from climbing her cheeks, she knew it was too late and she was already blushing.

He didn't kiss her but the pull was almost stronger because the wanting to kiss and not doing it hovered between them like an ache. "Is this the house?" he finally asked.

House? What house? Oh, right. She nodded. "Yes." That came out sounding reedy and unsure. She cleared her throat and tried again. This was her last hope. She had to talk him into this place or, since he wasn't a man who was ever talked into anything, had to present the house in the best possible light so he'd make a decision in its favor.

All her confidence began to dribble away. What had she been thinking? They'd looked at property so gorgeous her breath caught in her throat, and she'd wasted her last hope on a run-down house on a strange-shaped lot. He'd think she was deranged.

And she half thought he might be right.

But, fake it till you make it had helped her through more than one meeting with Rupert when she had no idea what was going on.

She grabbed the threads of her earlier confidence around her. "Okay," she said. "It's very different from everything we've looked at. But that's what I like about it. It's urban, funky. I'm not going to lie to you, this lot is a big challenge. It doesn't conform, it's a strange shape, and the shell of the current house will have to stay in order to retain the building envelope." She gulped in some air, realized she was forgetting to breathe, and forced herself to relax. "But, it's an amazing location, and, as crazy as this sounds, you can feel the happiness here. Luis—that's my roommate—his grandparents have lived her for fifty years. They are a big, happy family, and while I'm not into communing with the earth and rocks like you are, even I can feel the good energy."

He listened to her intently. Nodded. "Walk me around the lot," he said.

"Oh, right. Okay." She stepped outside with him and

took him on a tour of the entire property. That took about a minute. He didn't say anything. He could see the property markers the real estate agent had placed as well as she could.

"Hmm," he said.

Was hmm good or bad? Impossible to tell and she wasn't about to ask and take the risk of irritating him.

"Do you need some time alone out here?"

He hesitated. "No."

Oh, dear. He always sat in quiet and silence. Had he decided against her already?

"Do you want to see the interior?" she asked.

"Yes."

Okay, that had to be good. They went back inside and Luis came out of the kitchen with his grandmother. "Luis, this is Prescott."

The men shook hands and she could see them sizing each other up. Later she'd ask Luis for his impressions. He was smart about people. Luis introduced his grandmother and to her surprise, Prescott spoke to the woman in Spanish.

Luis's abuela smiled as though he'd given her a bouquet of roses and babbled back. Cool.

He seemed genuinely engaged with Luis's grandmother, not simply going through the vaguest of motions to be polite like he usually did when they were viewing a property. She could see that he was enjoying this woman and her home and it occurred to her that maybe Prescott wasn't distant with everyone, only with people who annoyed him or who wanted something from him that he didn't necessarily want to give.

Hope, and the sizzle of excitement that had gripped her when she'd first considered this house as a serious possibility, began to resurface.

She began to marshal the same thoughts and impressions that had excited her about this property when she first saw it, wondered how she might give him a tour that would show the place to its best advantage and then, with a flash of insight, realized that the best thing she could do would be to sit back and let Luis's grandmother show Prescott the house.

This was the woman who'd lived in it for half a century, who'd grown old here, who'd loved and raised children here. Maybe it wouldn't be the right approach in many cases for the current owner to show the home to an architect, but in this case, when she knew that Prescott went on instinct and some kind of spiritual voodoo to make a decision, maybe this lovely woman was exactly the person who should be showing off her home.

So, she and Luis hung back and let the grandmother talk. Prescott followed her from room to room, asked questions that she could tell even from her limited Spanish were about the light and weather patterns, and it seemed like he was asking about the neighborhood and the neighbors which seemed like a strange line of questioning and maybe she'd gotten that wrong.

The tour took half an hour. And then he sat in the kitchen with Grandma and Luis and Holly while they all drank coffee and ate more of the wonderful pan dulce.

She'd never seen him so charming. Luis's grandmother clearly fell half in love with him, and to her shock, Holly began to realize that she was half in love with him herself.

They were chatting about Mexico when there was a tapping noise on the kitchen window. Holly glanced up to see an exotic-looking bird staring in at their snack time, his head tilted to one side.

"Oh, Hector," Luis's grandmother said, rising from her seat. Then she spoke in rapid Spanish as she opened the window and the bird hopped right in and onto the kitchen counter.

"I hope you don't mind," she said, as she reached into a handy container and pulled out a handful of raw nuts. "His owners leave the window open sometimes and he comes visiting."

"Doesn't he fly away?" Holly asked, shocked that this pretty, colorful bird paid house calls to the neighbors.

"No. He never does. He visits with me, and then he flies back home. He's a parakeet and very smart." She sighed. "I'll miss Hector."

Meanwhile, the bird pecked away at the food and the older woman chatted away to him in Spanish. Then he half jumped, half flew onto her shoulder and nibbled at her gold earrings. She stroked his breast with one finger and then he stepped daintily onto the finger and was introduced to everyone. He bobbed his head up and down a few times which made them all laugh. Then she opened the window and the little bird flew back home.

How could you not love a place where exotic birds came to visit? She hoped Prescott agreed.

After a pleasant half hour, well, pleasant for everyone else it seemed, when it was all cake and coffee and parakeet visits and smiles and rapid Spanish that she couldn't follow, and her stomach was so nervous she could barely swallow the delicious cake, finally, finally, Prescott rose as though he had nothing more interesting to do than to sit around all afternoon chatting, but realized that Luis's grandmother was a busy woman with a house to pack.

Holly was surprised he didn't grab a box and start wrapping china.

He thanked Luis's grandmother for her hospitality and

kissed her on the cheek. Gave Luis a manly handshake and then said goodbye. She said her swift goodbyes, exchanged a hopeful glance with Luis, and followed Prescott out the door.

Knowing how touchy he was to be talked to when he was communing with nature or the land or the house spirits or whoever, she kept her mouth shut.

He walked to the end of the short path. Turned. Looked at the house. Walked the perimeter once more. Holly followed at a discreet distance, or as discreet as you can be on a small city lot. There weren't acres of oceanfront or landscaped grounds or forest for her to drop back to. She wanted to be in hearing distance if he said anything, but not in annoying distance.

He stood with his back to her, walked over to an old stone sundial and ran a finger around the edge.

Then he turned and walked to where she was standing. She tried to read some expression on his face but she didn't think there was one.

"Well?" she said when she couldn't stand it any longer.

He looked at her then. "I owe you a dinner out in a restaurant," he said. When she stood there staring at him, he said, "For our date. I promised you dinner and we never got there."

They'd been preoccupied with other activities as she recalled and dinner hadn't crossed her mind. When they were hungry they'd ordered in Chinese.

Now, she was torn to pieces by anxiety and he wanted to discuss dating. "Dinner? My entire future hangs in the balance and you're thinking about dinner?"

He cracked a smile then, as charming as anything he'd shown to Luis's grandmother and a whole lot more intimate. "To celebrate."

Her heart began to pound. "Are we celebrating some-thing specific?"

"You nailed it, Holly. I don't know how you did it, but this is it. This is what I've been looking for. Challenge, possibili-ties, an opportunity to really do a spectacular, sustainable design on a small lot."

She compared this quirky, mid-city lot with the stunning jewels of real estate he'd turned his nose up at. "This speaks to you?"

"This speaks to me."

She let out a whoop of joy and threw herself into his arms.

CHAPTER 11

He laughed. "Now you have to sell your boss. I doubt this is exactly the property that the Ruperts had in mind."

"You leave the Ruperts to me," she said.

She was happy she'd taken some psychology courses and negotiating in her MBA years because she was going to need every bit of persuasiveness to sell the Ruperts on The Mission.

In the end, she knew that all she had was Prescott. And the reasons he wanted to design a place on that particular lot.

She got on the phone to Iona, was put through two people and finally allowed to speak to her.

"Halle, you say you have good news. Tell me this means that Prescott is going to design my house?"

"That's exactly what I wanted to tell you," she gushed. "He's going to design you an urban retreat. He's very forward thinking, this is going to be the design of the future. Smaller footprint, completely sustainable." She suspected Iona didn't give a rat's ass about sustainability, she was the crown princess of conspicuous consumption, but one thing Holly counted on that she wouldn't be able to pass up on was fame.

"This design is going to be so forward thinking you'll be setting a trend. The big estates will be a thing of the past. This home will get as much media as you can stand. You'll be setting an example."

Iona didn't squeal with delight. She said, "Where is this place?"

Holly squeezed her eyes shut and held the phone away just in case. "Right in the center of San Francisco. The historical and exciting Mission district."

"The Mission? One of my housekeepers lives in The Mission." Close proximity to her staff did not sound like a big selling feature.

"Prescott's very excited about this project. If you don't want it, I think he's got a list of people waiting for him to design for them."

"Don't be hasty, Halle. I need to think about this. You lock that place up tight, sign something. Call my lawyer. I'll tell my husband to put some money down on it, and I will think about it."

"Absolutely."

Knowing that Iona needed more encouragement, and in love with the idea of setting her up as an example of living small and sustainably, she dragged up some of the skills she'd learned and, more importantly, the contacts she'd made in her publishing and media degree and let a hint of a rumor slip out. Soon, she suspected, Iona would be the poster girl of green.

❧

PRESCOTT SAID he'd take her to dinner at Brouix. In a city of fantastic restaurants, Brouix was in the top handful. She was thrilled to go there because she'd always wanted to, and because Prescott's firm had designed the interior. She knew from the website that the place was understated elegance, the design heavy on natural materials, bamboo and cork and granite.

Because working for Rupert occasionally required her to attend evening events, she'd supplemented her poor-grad-student-gets-her-first-underpaid-job wardrobe with a few nice pieces she'd purchased at her favorite vintage store.

She loved the owner's style and kind of liked that she was also dressing sustainably, in a recycled black dress that showed off her curves but in a subtle way.

Rupert hadn't bothered to contact her himself, but the former assistant had texted her when Iona had finally decided that she would take the property Prescott was willing to build on. "Boss happy. Think bonus. Buy yourself something nice."

So, she'd splurged, going to Maria's salon for a much-needed cut and style of her hair, indulging in a mani/pedi, and then she'd purchased a pair of shoes that were about twice what she'd ever paid for footwear in her life, but she considered them an investment.

At least, that's what she told herself.

Maria had worked magic with her hair, somehow taming the tangle into something sexy and feminine, and convinced her to try a red, red lipstick.

PRESCOTT HAD BEEN TICKING OFF ALL the items on his list that drove him crazy about Holly as he headed to pick her up in the limo. He liked driving, but his company had a limo service on retainer and he used it when he was going out so he could enjoy a drink or two and not have to either park his own car or worry about some kid in the valet parking taking control of his Tesla even for a minute.

In the quiet, sleek interior, he reminded himself that sleeping with Holly had been a dare. She'd shoehorned herself into his private life and then she'd behaved like a personal friend to him and to his entire family. He didn't quite know how he'd decided that taking her to bed was a priority in his life, but it had become one.

Now what?

Once was for fun and to satisfy that sizzle that had been between them since the first day he'd walked out of his office to discover her perched on top of his car like an over-sized and very untidy hood ornament.

Now he was taking her to dinner mainly as a celebration. He hadn't been as excited about a project for a while. Of course, she'd expect to end up back at his place. And until this moment he'd assumed the same. However, as the limo drew closer to her apartment, he wondered. It wouldn't be fair to raise expectations. She was a nice girl.

A really nice girl and they'd had more fun than he'd had in a long time. But she'd never be right for him in the long term. She had no restraint. He thought that was the biggest problem between them. He craved order and quiet and sleek aerodynamic styling. Holly was not quiet, or sleek, or orderly, and she most certainly wasn't aerodynamic. Her hair was all over the place. Okay, it was curly, so not entirely her fault, but he always fought the urge to tuck it behind her ears or something. And yet, when he'd held it in his hands when they were in bed together, the curls had felt silky and frothy. If laughter had a feel, it would feel like Holly's hair.

Her shirts were forever untucking from her skirts or pants. How hard was it to buy a shirt that fit? Immediately after he had the thought he felt like an ass. Easy for him to talk. He could afford to get his clothes custom made. Everything fit as though it had been made for him because most of his clothes had been made for him.

And yet other girls bought off-the-rack clothes and they weren't forever coming untucked. The collars of their shirts and jackets didn't end up so skewed that one side sat up and the other was folded down.

Her bag, her briefcase, always bulged with too much stuff. Her shoes weren't polished.

He realized that as much as he'd been looking forward to spending another night with Holly that he was going to have to tell her that their night together had been a one-time thing. Fantastic, enjoyable—when was the last time he'd laughed in bed and it had felt so good? But it wasn't fair to let her believe there was a future for them when there so clearly wasn't.

He'd made the decision, feeling a stab of regret but knowing he was making the right call.

Then they arrived at her apartment door. Since she'd been frank with him that her student loans were a big reason for her determination to keep a crap job with a crap employer, he hadn't been at all surprised to find that she lived in a poor looking apartment. Still, it bothered him that she lived here. She deserved so much more.

As the limo pulled up, he and the driver opened their doors at the same time. "I'll go to the door," he said, and got out. As he walked forward, the door to the apartment building opened and she stepped out.

It actually took him a moment to confirm that the gorgeous woman in front of him was Holly. Without her usual bags and electronics hanging off her, without any trails of clothing that needed tidying, she looked... It took him a second to come up with the correct word. Gorgeous, he realized. Amazing.

Someone, thankfully, had done something with that hair. It was cut into a style that made her curls work for her instead of against her. That hair gleamed with a decent cut that framed her face. Her make-up was nice. And when she smiled her red, red lips made him long to kiss her.

She wore a sleek black dress, much nicer than anything he'd ever seen her in before. Luckily, it was one piece, had no belts, collars or buttons that could be left open, dragging, hanging out or falling off. The dress showed off a figure he already knew to be spectacular, and that she tended to hide under the suits she wore for work.

Her shapely legs ended in shoes that his artistic eye approved of and his neatnik self applauded for being clean and shiny. He was almost certain those shoes had to be new, but he appreciated that for once nothing about her irked his sense of order.

Even her bag was small enough that not much of her traveling office could possibly fit into it.

"Wow, a limo," she said, with her big, friendly smile as he drew closer.

"You look beautiful," he said, because it was true and he was a man who appreciated beauty.

He saw her discomfort in the compliment when she shook her head quickly. Most of the women he dated took compliments as their due and knew exactly how beautiful they were. For many, their livings depended on their looks. So, it was fresh and kind of charming to see a woman blush and demur at a compliment.

In his mind, that little fluster made her more beautiful.

The driver had already stepped around and opened the door for her. She slipped into the limo, and, since she kept going, he slid in beside her.

"Did the Tesla run out of gas?" she teased.

"I thought this would be more relaxing. I never drink and drive."

"Good for you." Then she laughed. "I don't either, which usually means I take the bus or walk to wherever I'm going. A limo is a lot nicer."

Then she turned to him, her eyes gleaming. "She said yes."

He blinked at the rapid change of subject. "Who said yes to what?" But of course he already knew.

"Iona Rupert. I think she polled some of her friends and came back saying yes. She wants whatever house you design."

"She knows where it is?"

"Yep. I might have put a few ideas in her head, like how forward thinking she was to choose a smaller footprint, green technology house. How much media attention there would be. She lapped it up."

"Nice way to spin it."

"Thanks."

He wanted to keep his hands to himself but being beside her in the back of a town car, watching the excitement on her vivid face, he reached out and took her hand. Even her nails were painted and the soft feel of her skin beneath his palm reminded him of all the other soft parts of her.

When they sat down to dinner he enjoyed her enthusiastic pleasure in the place and the food. "I've never been here before but I'd heard how good it was. Your company did a great job. They must love you, too, because this has to be one of the best tables."

Holly didn't eat like a woman on a permanent diet. She didn't view food as her enemy and appear to count calories with every bite. She ate to enjoy.

When she took pleasure in all the flavors brought to them, he found his own enjoyment heightened.

"Do you really think the Ruperts are going to live in The Mission?" he finally asked, having trouble picturing Iona in the area.

Holly tilted her head to one side, "I imagine she'll drop that house into conversation to impress her friends more than she'll live in it. I picture the place being a kind of townhouse, one of many around the world, but no. I think she'll get her fabulous mansion somewhere. Now she's nailed down her Prescott Chance design, she'll soon want something bigger and more prestigious." She sipped her wine, looking guilty, like she might have said too much. "Does that bother you?"

"Of course it bothers me. I design homes that are meant to be lived in. But I made you a deal. You kept your end of the bargain. I'll keep mine."

"And there's the whole houses live longer than people argument," she reminded him. "Long after the Ruperts are dead, people will continue to live in that house and be part of its future."

"Now that you've got the property for them, I guess I won't be seeing so much of you." In his head he knew that was a good thing, but he was surprised at how much he was going to miss her.

She laughed. "Oh, you're not getting rid of me that easily. Rupert was very clear that I will be the point person on this project."

"The point person."

"Yes. I will carry plans and ideas back and forth."

"So, basically you'll be making decisions about someone else's house?"

"No. I won't be making any decisions. I'll be the go-between for information." She grinned. "Bringing you impossible demands. Going back with curt refusals that I will soften. You'll still be seeing a lot of me."

He reached across the table and stilled the hand that was fiddling idly with the remaining cutlery by placing his on top of it. "Good," he said.

As her head lifted and their gazes connected he knew he'd been lying to himself. He wasn't going to back away, not from this crazy but amazing woman who challenged him and made him laugh. Who kissed with her entire body and made love with the same honest enthusiasm she brought to most things.

He felt the slight quiver in the fingers trapped beneath his palm. "Prescott, what are we doing here?"

She was asking the same question he'd wondered about himself. The best answer he could give her was, "We're enjoying ourselves. It's simple and uncomplicated."

She seemed genuinely puzzled. "Nothing in my life ever ends up being simple and uncomplicated."

Having known her for a few weeks he could agree that was true but then she overscheduled herself, was too impulsive. He didn't share his thoughts with her, though. Instead he said, "Trust me. We can keep this from getting messy."

"Do you always manage to avoid entanglements?"

"I think so, pretty much."

She sighed softly. "Maybe you can show me how it's done."

He paid the check and they left together. When they got back to his place, he showed her exactly how it was done. Easy, uncomplicated.

"Are there rules to this?" she asked when they were taking a breather.

He frowned. "Rules to what?"

"Keeping things easy and uncomplicated? For instance, staying the night? Is that frowned on?"

He'd had absolutely no intention of spending the entire night with Holly. It was too soon for that. Maybe they'd get to that stage, maybe not. But even though the limo service had been warned they might be needed later, he found he had no interest in sending her home.

"No rules," he decided, leaning forward and kissing her.

CHAPTER 12

She shifted against him, fitting her body to his in a way that made him crazy with wanting the woman even though he was barely recovered from round one. "No rules. I think I can do that."

"So you'll stay the night?"

She grinned at him suddenly. "I packed a toothbrush and fresh panties."

It was far into the night when they fell into a sleep of exhaustion. Usually he preferred sleeping alone but he found himself curling his body around hers, as though he could protect her from the stresses in her life, protect her from the pair of sharks that were her employer and his wife.

He woke suddenly, realizing something wasn't right, and then noticed she wasn't in his bed any longer. He blinked at the clock. It was morning, but still early.

He rose slowly, stretched, and grabbed his robe out of the closet.

He padded downstairs, wondering where she was and walked in on an interesting sight. She had her back to him. She must have raided his wardrobe while he was asleep for she was wearing one of his white T-shirts, which hung nicely, barely covering her butt, showcasing her shapely legs.

She'd figured out the sound system and had some kind of pop music station on. She was dancing a little. The air was rich with the smell of the coffee he used. Her comfort with technology had paid off since you practically needed an engineering degree to operate his coffee machine.

And she was cracking eggs into a bowl, humming.

A rush of affection hit him. She seemed so happy, so at home in his kitchen. She was making him breakfast. He couldn't remember the last time a woman had cooked him breakfast.

"Smells great," he said.

She turned, as pretty in the morning light as she'd been last night. "I have never cooked in a kitchen that is so amazing. It makes me want to buy recipe books and experiment with exotic ingredients."

He walked up and hooked his arms around her, pulling her in for a long kiss. "Can you cook?"

She sent him her most appealing, impish grin. "If I had a kitchen like this, I could learn."

She could, however, make world-class eggs, a skill he complimented her on as he forked down the buttery soft scrambled eggs, the toast and fresh fruit. She even made coffee exactly the way he liked it. Industrial strength.

He was about to suggest a shower together when her phone rang. She glanced at it and as she was about to take the call, he said, "That guy treats you like a slave. I've a damn good mind to tell him what I think of him."

"Go ahead," she said, clicking through and offering him the phone.

It was a dare. A silent dare and Prescott wasn't one to

back off from a challenge which she should know better than anyone. He narrowed his gaze at her. Took the phone.

She let it go which suggested to him that she was as sick of Rupert calling her at all hours as he was.

He said, "It's Saturday morning and Holly is taking the weekend off which is her legal right."

Stunned silence greeted him. At least he supposed it was stunned since Alistair Rupert didn't seem like a guy who wasted time on silence. Then a voice he recognized said, "Darling? What are you doing answering Holly's phone?"

Holly's eyes were dancing as he stood there, busted.

"What are you doing calling it?" he countered.

His mother sighed. "I know you're right, she deserves a weekend off, but I accidentally deleted the RSVP list for the wedding. I'm sure Holly has a copy."

He handed the phone over and, as the conversation continued, discovered that of course his mom wanted so much more from Holly than a list.

He tried to read the paper and ignore the conversation, but he heard something about monogrammed cookies and room blocks and a gift table.

He turned a page noisily.

He raised an eyebrow when she got off the phone with his mother. She said, "I need fifteen minutes with this phone and then I'm yours."

"Fifteen minutes?"

"Yes."

He looked at her, wondering what she could possibly accomplish in fifteen minutes. It took him that long to settle to something and really engage his focus. She clearly misunderstood his expression for she snapped, "Promise. You can time me."

He decided he would.

As he watched, she pulled out her phone and began typing. Was she making notes? Texting? Impossible to tell. Then she made a call to the hotel where the overnight guests were staying. She managed to wheedle an extremely good block room rate and, he wasn't quite sure how she did it, but when she got off the phone, she'd talked the manager into supplying the hotel's shuttle bus to take guests to the wedding and bring them back to the hotel at no extra charge.

While he watched, she seemed to fan information and requests out to a larger network. "Iris. Monogrammed cookies, outsource?" she muttered aloud as she texted.

At thirteen minutes, she wrapped up and gave him a big smile.

"Okay. Good. That's under control."

"I have to ask. What did you do just now?"

She wrinkled her brow as though already forgetting. "Iris is making monogrammed cookies as a table favor, but Caitlyn thinks she's taken on too much and another baker can do them. Caitlyn's mother wants sugared almonds. Her family weddings have always included them and they are, apparently, good luck. So I sourced and ordered some."

"Why can't Caitlyn's mother do tha—"

"I get the feeling Caitlyn's mother is a little difficult."

"Great."

"I also confirmed the hotel room block, emailed your mom the RSVP list, confirmed the photographer and the minister and updated the checklist."

"I cannot believe you did all that in under a quarter of an hour."

She walked over and kissed him. "I am great at multi-tasking."

"And I am great at doing one thing at a time."

She sighed. "Yes, but my millions of things at once are pretty unimportant. Your one thing is that you design spaces that become part of history. You'll always be remembered. My multi-tasking?" She shrugged.

He pulled her down to the couch beside him. Gave her a quick hug. "My brother and his fiancée will never forget their wedding and my mom will never forget that you helped her. Maybe that's what you're really good at. Putting people and things together. Making it all work."

"So, you're saying we can't all be brilliant architects?"

"Somebody has to order the wedding almonds," he agreed with great seriousness, earning him a grin.

The phone buzzed again and he watched her struggle with herself before turning the damn thing off. "Don't you ever unplug?"

"No. It's my job."

"Nobody is supposed to work 24/7."

"One day, I hope to get promoted so I don't have to. I don't have the luxury you do, of going off and sitting in nature."

"Where would you go if you did?" he asked, finding himself curious. He was a creature of the land but, based on the properties she'd been showing him, she was drawn to the ocean.

"I love Point Reyes. I like to go there and watch the gray whales when they migrate or dolphins or seals or whatever's passing. Sometimes there's nothing and I watch the waves and the seabirds. I could stand at the lighthouse forever."

"Okay, that's an afternoon. What if you had, I don't know, a week?"

"An entire week? All to myself?"

"Unplugged," he reminded her.

The look she sent him suggested that was never going to

happen, but she played along like a good sport. "I think drive down the Pacific Coast Highway. Take the scenic route and stop at every little town I felt like stopping at."

"Have you never done that?"

"No. I always take the fastest freeway. I don't have time for a slow lane full of pretty views and clogged with tourists." She made a wry face. "That's kind of a metaphor for my life, isn't it?"

He nodded. "You miss a whole lot of pretty when you speed down the highway of life."

HOLLY FLOPPED on the couch with an untidy heap of bridal magazines scattered around her. Some had pages ripped out of them, some had colorful sticky notes protruding like multi-colored spines.

Maria walked in and immediately plopped herself beside Holly on the couch, grabbing one of the magazines with a sigh of pleasure. "Usually you're reading some boring business thing. This is so much better."

"This would look good on you," Holly said, pointing to the dress that had caught her eye the second Maria walked in. Traditional like Maria but also a little bit sexy.

She felt the wistfulness coming off Luis's girlfriend. "I would love to wear that dress. Heck, I'd love to get married. I don't even care if I wear jeans."

"Does Luis know?"

"We have to save enough money for the wedding first."

"I can plan your wedding for you. I'm brilliant at it. I think Caitlyn and Evan's wedding will be amazing. And I'd love to take on the challenge of making a magical wedding on a budget." She ripped out the page for Maria and handed it to her. Then went back to her reading, trying not to frown.

She felt Maria's gaze on her face but pretended she was riveted by the new and innovative uses for ivy in weddings. "I'm thinking of everything in indoor/outdoor terms. Getting married in October in the Pacific Northwest and hoping for a garden wedding is close to crazy, but that's what the happy couple wants, so we have to make something flexible enough to work in or out."

"Has he asked you?" Maria finally said.

"Has who asked me what?"

But they both knew.

"Has Prescott invited you to be his date for his brother's wedding?"

"No. But I didn't expect him to." Oh, okay, she'd really, really hoped that Prescott would ask her to be his date for his brother's wedding. She could admit this to herself even as it made her roll her eyes.

"He should invite you," Maria said. "You're seeing him, aren't you?"

"By seeing him, do you mean I've pestered him and practically forced him to agree to design a house for the boss I hate?"

Maria did one of those soft-voiced Spanish phrases that she suspected was an appeal to the saints. "No. I mean seeing him as in you went for dinner, in a limo, and you didn't come home for two days."

"You noticed that, huh?"

She nodded.

"Well, okay, we got close. But I don't think it means anything. I have to be practical about this. Prescott Chance is out of my league."

"No, Holly. He's not." She was quite serious.

She snorted. "Have you seen the guy? He's gorgeous and he's successful and he's rich, and, and..." She began flipping through the magazine, finally found the page she was looking for. A full page ad for the most exquisite underwear, modeled by the most exquisite looking woman, all dark hair and huge, mysterious eyes and a body that probably made the underwear look better than it did on its own. "That woman? She and Prescott used to date. She's Italian."

Maria swallowed, noisily. "That must be Photoshopped, or airbrushed or—no woman is that perfect." They both stared at the woman. She was ridiculously perfect. "How do you know he went out with her?"

"I researched him. I know as much as it's possible to know about that man without high-level government clearance." She sighed. "He dates supermodels and minor royalty and . . . and I'm this messy woman with freckles and scars on my legs from playing field hockey." She stared morosely at Seniorita Perfecto.

"She's probably an airhead," Maria decided.

"Do you think Prescott cares? Do men ever care about her brain if the woman on their arm looks like that?"

"Well, he's not going out with her anymore, is he?"

"He's not going out with me, either." She had to face facts. "I haven't heard from him."

"He didn't call?"

She shook her head, miserable.

"Oh, that's bad."

She nodded. After the two amazing days and nights with Prescott she'd fallen and hard. When he'd driven her home so she could get back to her overscheduled job, he'd kissed her goodbye and everything about the kiss said he'd call her. That they'd spend time together in the very near future.

And it hadn't happened.

"Then why are you looking at bride magazines?"

"I'm still helping his mom. And besides, I love doing it. Planning a wedding is so much more fun than organizing Rupert's calendar and doing the grunt work on deals that are designed to make Rupert richer and to screw over everybody else. It's not exactly a career to get warm and fuzzy about."

Maria stared at her. "You know what you should do? You should become a wedding planner."

Holly flicked another page. "I would love to do that. Can you imagine spending your life helping people create the perfect day? Making everything magical."

"Hey, I do enough hair on wedding days. Those are the most stressful days in the salon. Bridezillas and Momzillas and bridesmaids with PMS." She shuddered. "No thank you."

"Clearly, you have never worked for Rupert. Or Mrs. Rupert. Rupert is like all those monsters combined in one mean little package."

"You have all the qualifications. You can deal with difficult people, you can do a million things at once, and people like you."

"I don't know. Maybe I should."

They kept flipping pages and she could tell that Maria was falling under the spell of the magic of the bridal magazine. She had a bad feeling she was going to hear about it from Luis when he came in, but when he did, sweaty and limping from a soccer game in the neighborhood, he dropped his bag in the hall, kicked off his cleats and, seeing the two women on the couch surrounded by reading material said, "What's up?"

"Bride porn," Holly admitted, feeling a bit guilty.

"Really?" He limped over, gave Maria a kiss and said,

with his crooked grin, "Is there something you wanted to ask me?"

She giggled and blushed. "It's not for me to ask."

"Go on, you could get down on bended knee. I wouldn't mind."

"You're the one who has to get on bended knee," she reminded him.

He pointed to his knee, the source of the limp since he'd managed to tear all the skin off the knee cap. "Can't. You'll have to do it."

She smacked his shoulder. "Be serious. You need a shower." She grimaced as she looked at his wound. "And a bandage."

But later, when Maria had walked over to the market to buy dinner ingredients, which they usually did together, he made his knee the excuse for not joining her and Maria went alone. The door had barely shut behind her when he said, "Holly, what's going on?"

He was never usually serious so she had to adjust to a serious Luis. "What do you mean?"

"Maria and the wedding magazines. Is she really jonesing for a wedding?"

Holly started to reassure him that the magazines were hers, which they were, but when she thought back on the afternoon they'd spent, two girls poring over hairstyles and discussing floral arrangements and where they'd go on their honeymoon, she'd caught a real wistfulness coming from her friend. But Luis and Maria had been together a long time. Why was he asking her? "Don't you and Maria ever talk about this stuff?"

"Well, no. Not really. I mean, obviously we're together, and I love her, but I don't know. It's kind of been working okay as things are. I don't see a big reason to change the situation, you know? You're a great roomie and we're trying to save up. One day, I guess we'll get married." He talked the same way he would if he were talking about one day going deep sea diving or one day seeing the pyramids.

She realized, even as she opened her mouth, that chances were, if she told him what she suspected he needed to know, that she'd once more find herself looking for an affordable place to rent. But she liked Luis and she liked Maria and she liked them together.

"You know what I think? I think—what's a special place for you and Maria?"

He thought for a long moment. "She loves Twin Peaks, you know how you get up there and you can see the whole city and the bay. And at night. She loves to go there at night, when it's clear and you can see all the lights." He seemed uncomfortable telling her this, but she was only glad he'd been able to think of a place that was special to Maria.

"I think that if you were to dip into your savings and buy her a diamond ring and take her to Twin Peaks and, if you were to propose to her there, in a place that's already special to her, that it would be one of the happiest moments of her life."

He gulped. "You don't think she and I should start talking about it?"

"No. I don't. Maria's old-fashioned and romantic. She'd tell that story to her parents and her cousins and her girl-friends and her customers in the salon. And I think she'd say yes."

"Wow." He paced the main room of the apartment. It didn't take long. "You mean, like soon."

"Yeah, I mean, like soon."

"What about you?"

"No. Thank you. You're a great guy, but I don't want to marry you."

He threw a bridal magazine at her, and she ducked easily so it hit the wall with a splat. "I mean, you'll be losing the world's greatest roommate. What are you going to do about that?"

She was filled with affection for him, for Maria, for the wedding she was pretty sure she'd plan. She was really going to miss Luis. "Thanks for even considering me. It will take a few months to plan the wedding. That will give me some time to find a new place."

"Wow. You really think she's ready to get married, huh?"

She walked over and stood right in front of him. "Yes. I really do." Then she grinned. "But I'd make sure the ring was returnable."

CHAPTER 13

"Hi, Mom," Prescott said into the phone which he'd only picked up because it was his mother on the other end.

"I hope I'm not interrupting anything."

"You know you're not. Not even you get put through if I say no calls."

"Good."

"What's up?"

"I'm not sure what to do about Holly."

"Why do you have to do anything with Holly?" Sometimes talking to his mother was like figuring out Egyptian hieroglyphics. He was certain there was sense in there somewhere but it was work to pick through and find it.

"I mean about the wedding."

"Anything to do with the wedding and it's Holly you should be talking to."

"But that's what I'm getting at. I want to invite her. Would that be strange and awkward?"

He'd been working non-stop for enough hours that having a normal conversation with someone who was not an architect or designer was difficult. "Of course, she's coming. She's practically planned the damned thing."

He heard his mother's breath rush out in relief. "Oh, good. I was worried that maybe you hadn't asked her."

In point of fact, he hadn't asked her. It hadn't occurred to him that he needed to. Obviously, she was coming since, as he'd just reminded his mom, she'd practically planned the entire event, plus, he didn't want to turn up to the wedding solo. It seemed perfectly clear to him that they were going together. What was the big deal?

But when he got off the phone, he realized that his mother, like most women, didn't always come right out and say what she meant. More of those hieroglyphics. Perhaps, what she'd really meant was— No. The minute he started trying to figure out what she'd really meant he was hooped.

He picked up the phone he'd recently put down and made a call.

"Prescott Chance?" Holly's voice was full of surprise. "Is it really you?"

"What is with everyone today?" He glanced out the window but it was daylight. Impossible to see the moon. "Is it a full moon or something?"

"Maybe a blue one, since you're phoning me."

"I phone you," he said, feeling a little defensive since the only reason he had her number was that she'd programmed it in his phone when she'd snuck into his car.

"Prescott, I always phone you."

"Well, this time I'm phoning you."

"Oh. Is it about the site? Is there something you need?"

At the sound of her voice he realized he'd missed her. He hadn't seen her for a few days. He'd been working non-stop so she didn't know how far he'd got. "No. Nothing I need. I've done a preliminary design."

"Already?" she squeaked with excitement.

"Yes. That's how I work. When the site speaks to me, I usually get going right away." He found it so hard to explain that usually he didn't bother. He started feeling his way around the design and it began to appear almost like magic. There would be a great deal of hard work ahead, but when the design appeared, he worked in a white heat sketching, planning, calculating. He realized that he hadn't called her and it was rude. "I've been at it night and day," he added. "I get like this sometimes. I forget to eat. Barely sleep."

"You are such a creative genius." But the warmth was back in her tone, which he hadn't realized was missing until he heard it again. He felt his own warmth kindle.

"You want to come over and see my drawings later?" he teased.

"You know I do."

"Great. Come around seven. You can see the design and then we'll go grab some dinner or something."

There was a tiny pause, then she said, "Sure. Okay."

"Did you have other plans?"

"No. It's just that I guess I have to get used to the whims of a creative genius."

"I didn't mean..." He let out a breath. "I should have called." What an ass. "I'm sorry."

"No biggie. I'll see you at your place at seven."

SHE GOT HOME from work with barely time to shower and scramble into some fresh clothes. But she had to slow down when she raced into the apartment and found Luis there, obviously waiting for her.

"Hey, Luis. How was your day?"

"Good. I think." He seemed nervous. He rubbed his hands on his pants. Then he said, "I went shopping."

"Okay. Shopping is good." She hoped he'd remembered to get milk.

He reached into the battered canvas backpack he used instead of a briefcase. He pulled out a ring box. Handed it to her.

She gasped, with as much happiness and excitement as she hoped Maria would show. "Oh, my God. You did it."

"What do you think?"

She flipped open the box, her heart racing a little, because what woman's heart didn't race when a gorgeous guy presented her with an engagement ring? Even if the ring wasn't for her?

"It's perfect," she cried. A solitaire, as classy and traditional as Maria herself. "I think she'll love it."

"I'm picking her up in an hour." He took the ring box back from her. "Can't believe I'm doing this."

"I can't believe it either," she said. "Good luck!"

Of course, Prescott, being a man, had not bothered to tell her where they were going for dinner. She had no idea if they were heading to some fancy place where she might run into a movie star or whether they were grabbing take-out sushi. She dressed in her best jeans, the new shoes and a silk top.

She drove over to his place feeling a quiver of excitement. He hadn't lost interest in her. In fact, he'd been engrossed in his work. She'd heard in his voice the moment when he realized that he'd been rude. A man who could see his fault and apologize frankly for it was a man she felt she could trust. So, she gave him some slack.

And she gave him a whole lot more slack when she saw the design.

Naturally, architects all used computers. Naturally, Prescott liked to do his first pass with pencil. Or charcoal or something an artist might use, so what she saw first was hand-drawn sketches.

She fell in love immediately. "This is amazing," she said.

"I had to be creative to keep the shell of the old building," he explained. But he'd kept the envelope and made something beautiful.

"This is like really high-end recycling," she said, feeling her enthusiasm bubble. "Old meets new."

"I'm designing it so it's as green and sustainable as modern materials will allow."

"What's this?" she asked, pulling out a more detailed black-and-white drawing. "Isn't this the existing house?"

He glanced over. "Yes. I started with a detailed rendering of what was there. It helps me sometimes to draw the existing building. It gives me ideas."

"But you've signed it."

He looked slightly uncomfortable, a look that was pretty new on him. "I'm going to have it framed and give it to Luis's grandmother. I'll keep a photocopy for myself.

In that moment, as she stared at the drawing he'd made to give to the people who were leaving that home, leaving part of their hearts behind in it, she fell in love with him.

Falling in love was one of those expressions she'd heard her whole life. Songs trumpeted the notion, people talked of falling in love all the time. But she'd never actually imagined that a person could quite seriously tumble. One minute she was walking along on her emotional road, which might meander a bit but was a fairly flat, scenic route, and then she'd taken an unwitting step and the road disappeared. She'd gone sailing off a cliff, falling. Falling.

The trouble with falling in love was that she had no idea if the fall ended in any kind of safety net.

All she knew was that she was dizzy with the drop.

"Are you okay?"

He was looking at her with concern and she realized that something of her feelings must have shown on her face.

"Yes. Yes. It's just that..." She looked at him, at this man that she'd so foolishly and accidentally fallen in love with. "Prescott, that's the nicest gift they could have."

"If they don't like it they can toss it in a dark closet."

"I guarantee that it will hang in a place of pride."

"We can invite them to the opening when the new home's finished."

She giggled. "Can you imagine them mingling with Rupert's friends?"

"I know who the classier couple will be. So," he said as he pulled back, "what do you feel like eating?"

"I'm not fussy."

"Would take-out be all right?"

Good thing she'd dressed for all possibilities. "Yes. Take-out would be fine."

"Good. I want to sit on the site and watch the moon."

And he'd asked her if it was full? She felt like asking him the same question.

It was actually kind of nice to sit on the grass and eat sushi. Luis's grandparents had already moved and Prescott had a key, of course, but he didn't want to see inside the house. He wanted to watch the moon and feel whatever spooky things he needed to feel. And she was content to sit and munch sushi and wonder where she was going to find a new place to live.

Prescott was a relaxing person to be with. He didn't talk much, mostly seemed to be in his own world.

She pulled out her tablet and began making notes.

"You working?" he asked after a few minutes.

She glanced up. "No. I'm making notes for Marie and Luis's wedding."

He shook his head, his dark, dark hair moving in a way that made her want to put her hands in it and feel the silky strands. "More weddings?"

"He's asking her tonight. I'm so excited."

"What is it with girls and weddings?"

"I don't know. I think secretly we all want to be a princess at least once. So, you get to wear a great gown and hopefully have a great guy stand beside you and tell the world he's going to love you forever, to be there for you. It's pretty seductive."

"Speaking of weddings, I'm driving to Hidden Falls Friday. Thought I'd leave around three. Can you get away then?"

She stared at him. "Prescott, I haven't been invited to your brother's wedding."

"Don't be ridiculous. You're my plus one. Obviously."

She felt like hitting him over the head with her computer tablet, might have done it if she didn't think the trauma would permanently damage her electronics. In a dangerously calm voice, she said, "And why would I assume I was your plus one?"

"Because I, well, we..." His tone petered out. "I didn't think you needed a formal invitation. You've pretty much planned the entire show. And you and I are, well, we're—"

"What? What are we, Prescott?"

In frustration he roared, "We're sleeping together."

"Do you take every woman you sleep with to family weddings?"

"Never had one before." Then he slumped back. "No.

You are unique in every way. The first woman I've ever introduced to my family that anyone actually liked."

"Well, that's nice of them."

"Come off it. Will you go to Evan and Caitlyn's wedding with me?"

"As your plus one?"

"As my date?"

"Yes. And thank you for asking me."

"So, would Friday at 3 be okay with you? I thought we'd take our time and drive up."

"Fine. But I will have to work in the car. Is that a problem for you?"

Of course it was a problem. He liked to think while he drove, or listen to decent music, or simply talk to Holly. But if he said anything she'd take her own car and the thought of her driving that heap of junk, never mind taking business calls while she was driving it, seemed too harrowing to risk. "No. It's not a problem."

She sent him that twisted grin that was one of his favorite things about her. "Liar," she said softly. "But thanks."

So, they drove up together while she dealt with bankers, other minions in the Rupert empire, Rupert himself three times, and once, jarringly, his mother.

"Your mother says, 'Hello'" she informed him when she got off the phone and onto one of her electronic note takers.

"My mother called you to say hello to me?"

"No. She called me about the ring bearer's pillow."

"The ring bearer's pillow?" He thought he could have gone his entire natural life without ever knowing such a thing existed.

"Yes. She thought we didn't have one, but we do."

"You think of everything."

"Funny, that's what she said. Only when she said the words they didn't sound sarcastic."

"It's not you. It's weddings, I guess. Who needs all that fuss and hoopla? For a dying institution that fails fifty percent of the time."

"How can you be so cynical when your own parents are the poster couple for a happy marriage?"

"I just don't see the point."

"Is that part of your clutter-free philosophy? No messy relationships?"

"You make it sound like that's a bad thing."

"No. More kind of sad. Messy can also be interesting and connected."

He had lots of time to watch what she meant by connected when he saw her once again in the thick of his family. If you wanted interesting, messy and connected, you had no further to look than the Chance family on the eve of their first wedding.

But this time he'd done a little advance planning. He'd called up his sister Iris and pretty much begged her to shack up with her boyfriend for the weekend so that he and Holly could stay at her house.

"And why would I do that for you? When there are so many other deserving relatives who would love to use my house for the weekend?"

He racked his brains for an answer. "Because I'm your favorite brother?"

She laughed. Didn't deny it, but didn't agree either.

"Because, the next time you come to San Francisco shopping you can use my place." In fact, she always used his place, but he thought it would be too obviously pressuring her if he mentioned that.

In the end she agreed so easily that he half thought

they'd already hatched that plan in the grand scheme of things. Still, he was happy to have somewhere to stay that didn't involve a long drive since he'd already determined that he and Holly in the bunk room was not an option.

Pleased with his advance maneuvering, he drove straight to his sister's. Holly was busy juggling phones—he'd realized on this memorable trip down that her mobile office included not one, but two cell phones. One of which was strictly so Rupert could have her on call at all times.

He hated the way she always took a quick, shaky breath before answering the Rupert phone, and he hated even more the barking tone he heard coming through loud and clear.

And he was designing a house for this moron? He must be crazy.

It wasn't until he'd pulled to a stop in front of his sister's Victorian that Holly finally put her toys away and glanced around. She blinked a few times and rolled her neck, then asked, "Where are we?"

"This, my dear guest, is where you and I will be staying for the weekend."

She didn't look delighted. "You mean, we're not staying with the rest of the family?"

"Here's the deal. If I am spending an entire weekend with you, there will be sex involved. And sex and the bunk beds in my old room just aren't going together in my mind."

She sent him that mischievous glance that told him something outrageous was about to slip out of her mouth. "Too bad, I had some ideas."

In spite of himself he started to get interested. "Ideas about sex? In the bunk beds?"

"Mmm-hmm. I think bunk beds offer certain possibilities to people of reasonable flexibility."

"How's your flexibility?" he had to ask.

She grinned at him. "A lot better than reasonable."

He kissed her, because how could he not? Then whispered a few suggestions in her ear about what he could do with a decent bed and privacy.

Her lips were wet when they drew apart and her eyes had gone misty. "Okay," she said softly. "Your ideas might work too."

With a chuckle, he unfolded himself from the car and began dragging out bags. She packed pretty seriously for a weekend, he thought, until she stopped him. "Not that big red bag. Or the paper shopping bags. Those are all for the wedding."

"What are you now, UPS?"

"I loved helping plan this wedding. And in San Francisco, I had access to so much great stuff. Caitlyn has zero shopping options in Miller's Pond, and your mom has even fewer in Hidden Falls."

"They both have access to the Internet and my mom only has to drive an hour or two to get to some pretty substantial shopping."

"I wanted to do it," she said. "It was fun."

How anyone could have fun unearthing a pillow for a ring bearer was beyond him. But he didn't comment, merely avoided the wedding-related bags and hefted the others.

CHAPTER 14

*I*ris had the door open by the time they'd loaded up all the bags. She met them with her big smile and hugs for both of them.

"Come on in. Kettle's on."

"Thanks, but I should get straight over to your parents' place," Holly said.

"No point. Mom's at the hairdresser. I've got literally half an hour and then I'm heading back to the bakery. I've got extra staff working to get everything ready for tomorrow. It's been so much fun I might seriously add catering to my business."

"You know, that is such a great idea. You'd really improve your profitability without hugely affecting your costs of doing business. Obviously, you've already got the premises, the industrial kitchen and a lot of the supplies." Holly said, immediately switching from wedding planner to MBA business consultant. How she switched so many roles so fast was way beyond his comprehension.

"Exactly, and there is not only no decent restaurant in town, but there isn't a caterer for thirty miles."

"Cool. If you want to run a business plan by me, I'd be happy to take a look."

"Seriously? That would be great. My biggest worry is staffing. I've already got two coffee shops and . . ." She faltered for a second and then went on, "If I wanted to slow down a bit personally, if I started a family or something, then—"

"Started a family?" He couldn't believe what he was hearing. "Are you seriously planning to have kids? After basically being the stand-in mom for all the younger kids?"

Iris shrugged, her eyes holding a smile. "I loved it. I love kids. So, yes. If things work out, I am planning a family."

"Does that mean that you and Geoff?" Holly jumped in.

His sister nodded. He wanted to be happy for her, and he was, but he wasn't sure he could stomach another wedding. Not for a while. But then, everybody from celebrities to no-name Joes had kids without getting married these days. Maybe she'd save them all the hassle and herself the trouble and skip the wedding part. Even as he congratulated her silently on being sensible, she leaned in to Holly and said, "And I am seriously hoping you'll help plan the wedding."

They giggled and hugged and he was glad that the tea kettle whistled at that moment so Iris could jump up and break the sorority party.

He had no idea why he felt like he was choking the more the wedding planning went on. It was starting to feel like an epidemic. First Evan, then Holly's roommate Luis and his girlfriend, now Iris. It wasn't that he cared about other people getting married. It was the look on Holly's face that made him feel as though there wasn't enough air in the room.

However, after tea and a selection of Iris's amazing

brownies and lemon bars, she helped them carry the bags upstairs to her bedroom. While Holly was busy thanking her, and he was thinking how smart he was to have scored a quiet place for the two of them, Holly suddenly gasped.

He glanced up to find her staring at the wall.

He followed her gaze and his sister must have done so too for she walked over to it. "Yes, my very own Prescott Chance original." He'd done the artist's rendering of her house when she first bought the place. Nice that she'd given it pride of place above her bed.

When she'd shown them where everything was, Iris said she had to get back to work. Holly glanced at him and said, "Is it okay if you take me to your parents' place now?"

"Yes. Sure."

When they pulled up at the house he'd grown up in, he felt for a second like he was in the wrong place. There were people everywhere.

Some burly guys with a van were hauling out a huge tent. Since Holly had been checking the forecast as anxiously as though it was her own wedding, he knew that there was dry weather in the forecast.

As they stepped out of the car, another van pulled into the drive behind them. This one had a florist/outdoor store logo on the side panel. A couple more burly young guys got out and opened the back, then they started hauling trees in pots— trees in pots?—toward the front door.

Holly bolted past him and headed the guys off. "Follow me," she said. "The trees are going in the back garden."

Shaking his head, he walked to the house. His mother was wandering around with a clipboard and a new hairstyle, looking like she needed a few hours in her mediation yurt. She was on the phone when he walked in and waved to him distractedly before making more notes on her clipboard.

He found his father muttering over the electrical panel. Jack Chance was one of the finest men Prescott knew. But as a handyman, well, he had a lot more enthusiasm than talent.

"Dad," he said. "What's up?"

"Your mother wants a lot of twinkle lights in the back yard for when the sun goes down. Trouble is I'm not sure they won't blow a fuse."

Or burn the entire house down.

"You know, Dad, one thing about being an architect is that I've learned a lot of building skills along the way. Want me to take a look?"

The patent expression of relief on Jack's face said it all. But he remained casual. "Yeah. That'd be great, if you don't mind."

So, Prescott rolled up his sleeves and got to work.

As the evening progressed he watched Holly, the way she was the one they turned to when things went wrong or there were questions. She either knew off the top of her head or she pulled out her tablet and had the information at her fingertips. She was the one who'd organized the block of rooms at a hotel an hour away, and it was she who'd come up with the idea of a shuttle for the guests. She seemed to be everywhere at once. Counting tablecloths, helping Marguerite with the flowers, talking about traffic flow with Iris.

By the time everything was ready for the big event the next day, it was late and everyone was tired.

That's when Evan walked in with half a dozen pizza boxes. Prescott didn't think he'd ever been so glad to see his brother.

"Where's Caitlyn?" Cooper asked, a smudge of dirt creasing his face. He'd been assigned to haul the potted trees around while Prescott and Jack wired up the twinkly lights.

"Caitlyn's doing whatever brides do the night before the wedding." Evan shrugged. "She's got her mother and her best friend with her. We won't see her until tomorrow."

"Well, that sucks," Cooper said, helping set pizza boxes out on the big table, while Daphne and Holly brought out plates and napkins and a couple of huge pitchers of ice tea to go with the cold beer that Evan also provided.

"It's bad luck for the groom to see the bride the night before the wedding," Daphne explained.

"How are you holding up?" Jack asked his son.

Evan seemed to think about it. Nodded a few times. "Good. I feel good."

"Nervous?"

"Sure. I'm nervous that I'll screw up somehow, and let her down. I can't believe I got so lucky, you know?"

Jack nodded sagely. "I do indeed know. To be honest with you, I still feel that way about your mother."

They flipped open the pizza boxes and chowed down. All the hard work had made him hungry and somehow restless. What was it with the wedding fever? And why did he feel like he was the only one who didn't have it and yet he was the one feeling out of sorts?

"Are you okay?" Holly asked as they drove back to Iris's place. "You were so quiet at dinner."

"In the pandemonium of dinner at the Chances you noticed one person being quiet?"

She reached for his hand. "I always notice you," she said.

It was simply said, and he knew that she meant the words. Which made him feel hot and prickly all over. Why had he ever agreed to let this woman into his life in the first place? He still recalled seeing her perched on top of his car.

How had he not realized the obvious? A woman who would sit on a complete stranger's car and accost them was not someone who was going to be easy to get rid of.

But had he? Had he gotten rid of her when it would have been relatively easy?

Hell, no. He'd taken the craziest challenge in the universe, wasted precious time looking at building sites so he could build a home for two loathsome people he didn't remotely want as clients.

All because of Holly.

And had that been enough? Had worming her way into his professional life been enough?

Hell, no.

She'd also barged into his family home, inserted herself into wedding planning, and somehow found her way into his bed.

Now everything was weddings, and she was in the middle of it, Holly Legere, Wedding Planner to the Chances.

"I'm never getting married."

There. He'd said it. Don't bother throwing a bridal gown net over my head or a noose of rosebuds round my neck and a damned ring bearer's pillow to suffocate me with. Not going to happen.

His words came out sharper than he'd intended and the effect was that she pulled her hand away from his. "Okay," she said, mildly.

And the instant her hand left his he wanted it back. And felt like an ass. He pulled to a stop in front of his sister's place and turned to Holly. In the dim light, she looked mysterious. "Sorry. I didn't mean to snap at you. I just don't know what the hell's wrong with everybody. I spent an entire evening putting twinkle lights in a bunch of rented trees so my brother can make a fool of himself."

"Maybe your brother doesn't see it that way."

"Of course, he doesn't. Everybody's caught up in wedding fever. But not me. I'm telling you right now, don't get any ideas. I am never getting married."

For a long time she didn't say anything, then, instead of screaming at him, or stomping out of the car or slapping him or something, she quietly said, "Who hurt you?"

And it wasn't she who stomped out of the car, it was him.

HE DIDN'T EVEN KNOW where he was going until his feet turned onto a path that would take him out of town and into the forest. He could hear her following him and so he lengthened his stride. He did not want her following him, bothering him, trying to save him. Couldn't she accept that?

He got to a dirt trail that people walked their dogs on. If he kept going, he'd join old logging roads and trails that led hikers and climbers into the mountains.

There was a pain in his chest and when he reached an old-growth fir, he stopped to rest his back on it, catching his breath.

He thought Holly would have turned back but no, here she came, hurrying after him like an angel of mercy he didn't want or need.

"Leave me alone," he snapped when she grew closer, a vague shape in the near darkness, her breathing labored.

"No." She said it simply. "No. I won't leave you alone."

He turned back and ahead all he saw was the trail leading into darkness.

She came behind him and wrapped her arms around him, resting her cheek between his shoulder blades. "Who hurt you?" she asked again. Softly.

"The people who gave birth to me, I think." He'd never spoken of this, not to anyone, and standing there, he didn't have the strength to keep it all inside anymore.

"Oh, Prescott." That's all she said. She felt warm against him and it was cold and dark on the path he was on, so he turned back, held her against him, and talked.

"I do remember. Not much. Like shadows. Nightmares. But I'm pretty sure they're memories. Some people shouldn't be parents. Mine were like that. I don't remember much, but I know they put me outside if I was noisy or misbehaved. To punish me. I can still hear the sound of the lock turning against me."

"Oh, my God," she said.

"I think one night they forgot I was out there. I remember being scared, and puny and crying. I think I tried to walk to a neighbor's and got lost. I remember falling down and then sitting by this huge tree. And, I don't know, it sounds stupid, but I felt connected. I knew I was going to be okay. Something was looking out for me. So, I just stayed there."

"All alone? At night?"

"I don't remember. It's fuzzy bits and pieces. A light in my face. A place that had a huge wooden counter and smelled funny. Hospital? Police station? No idea. Then my next memory is digging in the earth, helping Daphne plant something. Beans maybe. She was smart enough, even then, to get me in the dirt. Part of the land. It's always healed me."

"But not people."

"I learned not to count on anyone. So I don't."

"Oh, poor little boy," she cried. "Poor, poor little boy." She pulled him to her. Strangely, when he'd only meant to push her away, to explain the darkness that lived inside him, he found himself pulling her to him, hard.

"It's cold," he said, feeling her shiver. The day had been warm, but it was early October and the night was cold. They walked back holding hands.

They talked then, most of the night.

"Do Daphne and Jack know how much you remember?"

He shook his head. "They've never pushed. I know I used to have bad nightmares. It was a lot later that I figured out they were memories. I'm not going to whine. They've been great. Not many kids who start out like me end up so lucky. Who am I to whine?"

"Prescott, you were hurt. The people who should have loved and cared for you pushed you away when you were most vulnerable. It's okay to hurt."

"Mostly, I don't."

"You don't let people get close, either, do you?"

It made so much sense to her now. The way he was more comfortable out on the land on his own. He trusted the land. It had saved him.

She loved this man. Could see all the good in him, all the passion and potential, but if he stayed blocked off, refusing to let her in, what hope was there for her?

She'd imagined the biggest obstacle between them was his wealth and position. How wrong she'd been. He used those things to help distance himself from other people. The real obstacle was his own inner demons.

She could fight a lot of things. She was a resourceful woman. But she didn't think she could fix what ailed Prescott, not if he wouldn't face up to his problems. Together, she thought they could fight his demons into submission, but all on her own? She didn't have a chance.

When they finally went to bed he held her with a sweetness that held an edge of desperation. She gave him everything she had to offer. Her body, her comfort, her love, even though she knew he didn't want to face that she'd fallen in love with him.

She wondered if he'd ever be able to love her. If he'd ever let himself be that vulnerable? And on that thought, she finally fell asleep.

HE HAD NEVER TOLD anyone about his early memories. As Prescott watched Holly sleep, he wondered why she, of all people, should be the one to dig those deep-buried secrets out of him. In sleep, she lost the lines of strain that being at Rupert's beck and call had put there. Her cheeks were round, her lips full. The half circles of her lashes looked like shadows under her closed eyes. And that hair, it was a halo of fire and light.

He knew he wouldn't sleep, so he settled beside Holly and let himself be comforted by her presence.

He wasn't a fool. He knew, of course, that whatever had happened to him in those first early years of his life, whether he remembered them or not, had messed him up but good. He'd been okay with his isolation. Fine knowing he could never truly trust anyone but himself. He loved his family unreservedly, but he was his own man, always had been. To let a woman into his life in a serious way wasn't something he was sure he could do. A woman like Holly, for instance, wouldn't take what he could give. She'd always want more. She'd want everything and he wasn't sure he could give it. Not to her. Not to any woman.

The sensible thing to do would be to part. For her sake.

THE WEATHER, as Holly had so hoped, cooperated with the wedding plans. Not that she'd played a huge role, but it was nice to see that her suggestions had been taken and that Caitlyn and Daphne and Iris had respected her talents and given her full rein. Organizing a million things into one coherent whole was a talent she'd never thought much of until she'd worked for Rupert and learned the value of juggling a hundred balls at once. It wasn't only keeping them in the air that was tough, but they were different sizes and weights and some shot fire and some contained live ammunition. And then, she'd think, okay, I can manage, and he'd throw in a helium balloon to keep her on her toes, followed by a medicine ball.

And she hadn't dropped a single ball. Not once.

Maybe she didn't love Rupert or have huge respect for him or his company, but he'd taught her the value of her own skills and that was something. So, she'd had complete confidence in offering to take on some of the organizational burden of the wedding and when she saw how smoothly everything went, she was pretty pleased with herself.

Rupert, the notorious skinflint, had come through with a surprisingly generous bonus once he had Prescott. She'd used some of it to buy herself a new outfit for the wedding. Her dress was a soft green that paired with a lacy cream jacket. She'd found matching shoes and, since she didn't want to waste money on a new purse, decided to forego one. Which meant she had nowhere to stick her cell phone.

Which meant Rupert couldn't get hold of her.

Hopefully, he was asleep in another time zone anyway, so she put him out of her mind and prepared to enjoy the day.

She and Prescott hadn't referred to his revelations of the night before. She knew he needed time to sort out his feelings but she also felt real hope that he'd shared something so intimate with her. Maybe it meant he had feelings for her. She hoped so more than she believed it. And yet, she kept feeling his gaze on her as she helped the little ring bearer, Cody, to practice walking up the aisle with the pillow, or when Daphne, stunning in a new blue dress, called her over for a quick consultation. When she caught his gaze she felt such a confusing mess of emotions inside him that she wanted to walk over and pull him into her arms and tell him everything would be okay. But, of course, she didn't. Mostly because she wasn't sure things would be okay.

CHAPTER 15

Caitlyn's mother and father arrived before the bride and within minutes there was trouble. The mother was cold and beautiful and, unfortunately, also wearing blue. She guessed nobody had suggested the mothers consult each other on their outfits. Holly made a mental note to add that detail to any weddings she planned in the future.

Caitlyn's mom stepped onto the lawn as though it were a farmer's field and she was afraid of stepping on cow dung. The glance she flicked at the house was full of disdain. Oh, dear.

Evan did his best, going forward to welcome them and introducing Jack and Daphne to their soon-to-be in-laws. She could see that Caitlyn's parents were looking down their noses at the Chances as though they were yokels.

"Go over there," she said, clutching at Prescott's arm, clad in an Armani summer-weight suit. "Let them see that their daughter is marrying into Prescott Chance's family."

He glared down at her. "I hate snobs."

"I know that," she said, frustrated. "But you love your parents, don't you? You have to rescue them."

"Oh. Okay. Come with me." And he dragged her over to the awkward group.

Evan greeted them like the lifesavers they were.

When he introduced them to Eunace and David Sorenson, Caitlyn's father said, "Prescott Chance the architect?" as though wondering how a famous architect had sprung from such uninteresting people. She could see that Daphne was looking upset and Jack belligerent.

"Isn't it a beautiful day," Holly said to Caitlyn's mom.

"Not for me it isn't." There was a heavy sigh. "I had such high hopes for my daughter."

"Now just a minute!" Jack began.

"Jack, please," Daphne said.

And then, to everyone's horror, Caitlyn's mother began to cry.

There was a moment of stunned awkwardness. But Holly hadn't worked for Rupert all these months and not learned how to deal with difficult people. She said, "Let's go inside. I'll get you some ice tea."

Once inside, she took Caitlyn's mother into the den where she was certain they wouldn't be disturbed, and then she simply listened to the complaints of a woman who didn't seem to understand her own daughter or particularly want her happiness. It seemed to Holly that all she wanted was to enlarge her own ego. "She had so much potential. She was one of the best surgeons in New York City. She was being groomed for better things. Why, she could have ended up as surgeon general of the United States with our connections and her talent." The woman sniffed and sipped delicately from her glass of tea. "She had such a future ahead of her. And the men she dated were all Ivy League, you know.

Young men of distinction. But she threw it all away to be a country doctor and marry a small town attorney." She sniffed again. "My only daughter. Such a disappointment."

Holly thought about how happy Caitlyn and Evan were and how clearly unhappy this woman was, and managed to stifle her irritation. For Caitlyn and Evan's sake she was determined to get this woman on their side. So, she played to the woman's ego. She said, "I know how hard it can be, but my boss, Alistair Rupert, always says, 'Whenever you're in public, never let them see you cry.'" In fact, his actual words were, "Never let them see you with yer knickers down," but she reworded it for Caitlyn's mother.

As she'd imagined, her shameless name dropping worked. "You work for Alistair Rupert?"

"Yes."

"I don't suppose he's coming to the wedding?"

"Unfortunately, no. He's in London."

The woman sighed, as though it was just one more disappointment in a life full of them. Then she put down her drink with a snap. Opened her clutch purse and touched up her lipstick. "All right," she said, pulling her shoulders back. "I may not like it, but I'll do my best."

And Holly returned her to the wedding, one crisis averted.

As she socialized with the guests, while also keeping a surreptitious eye on the schedule and the interpersonal dynamics, Holly found herself approached by a woman about her own age with a shining waterfall of perfect blond hair and a sun-catching smile. "Hi, Holly right? I'm Virginia Lewisham. Daphne says you're the wedding planner."

She shook her head. "No. I'm really not. I helped out a little, that's all."

"Daphne says you worked miracles. Listen, I'm getting

married in six months. I haven't had time to plan anything. I didn't even know what kind of wedding I wanted until I got here. But this is it," she said, gesturing to the surroundings. "It's perfect. Casual and elegant at the same time. Are you interested in planning my wedding?" She lowered her voice. "I'm an only child so let's just say the budget will be generous. Your biggest task would be to make sure I don't end up with something huge and ostentatious."

"I have a full-time job. I'm sorry. I wouldn't have time."

The woman handed her a business card. "Think about it. If you change your mind, or if you know someone who could do something as amazing as this, where people can feel relaxed but still everything's done right, then I'd love to hear about them."

"I will," she said.

And wouldn't she a thousand times rather plan weddings than run around after Alistair Rupert?

She ducked back into the house to put the card with her things and—okay, she couldn't go all day without checking messages, she was too well-programmed. When she checked her phone, she discovered a message from Alistair Rupert. Her heart sinking, she listened to the voice mail. He never bothered identifying himself since this phone was a hotline straight to her. Nor did he ever waste time with pleasantries. The message went like this: "Iona's got preliminary architectural drawings for the house. She wants to see it tomorrow. I'm flying in tonight. Meet us at the site at noon." No, sorry to bother you on a Sunday, no hope you're not busy or in another city for a wedding. Typical Rupert.

And, even as she fumed, she panicked. It was a nine-hour drive from Hidden Falls to San Francisco with no stops, delays or accidents.

She ducked out to find Prescott and told him about the message.

"That guy's a dick," he said.

"I know. But you don't say 'No' to Alistair Rupert, not if you want to stay employed." She felt her brow wrinkle as she tried to figure out a plan. "I can't ask you to leave your family wedding. I'll get a flight tomorrow morning. There must be something."

To her surprise, he pulled her against him and gave her a quick, one-armed hug. "I am not letting that troglodyte near my design without me being there. We'll go together."

"Really? But we'll have to leave today, the second the wedding's over."

He shook his head. "No. We'll both fly down. Believe me, Cooper will be only too happy to drive my car back to me. Or James." He thought for a second. "Pretty much every guy here would drive that car down for me."

She breathed in and out once. Fast. "Okay. Thank you."

"And Holly? I've got this one. I'll get us flown down there."

"But your plane is—"

"Like I said, I've got this one."

The relief of letting him take some of the stress of her shoulders was unbelievable. She leaned up on tip-toe and kissed his cheek. "Thank you."

"We're in this together," he told her.

After that, everything happened so fast. Caitlyn arrived, looking beautiful in a wedding gown that was simple and stunning. She looked so happy, and when she and Evan stood together and said their vows, they were so deeply in love that Holly felt her eyes mist. To her surprise, Prescott reached out and gripped her hand.

Then there was food and speeches and as the day faded,

all those twinkle lights that Prescott had complained about added a sense of magic.

She had no idea when he did it, but by the time they left that night, he told her they had a plane booked for nine in the morning.

Holly kissed Prescott goodbye when his limo service dropped her off at her place. Then she raced around, gathering every bit of data she'd collected for her sales pitch to the Ruperts on why a small house in The Mission was going to be perfect. Even as she showered and dressed, she rehearsed arguments that sounded completely great if she were pitching to people who cared about the earth, community, culture and integrity. Since she was pitching to the Ruperts, all she had was that this was the house Prescott was willing to design for them.

She'd begged him on the ride back to try a little harder to be nice to the Ruperts but her hopes weren't high.

Oh, well. They'd paid a deposit to secure the property, they'd seen Prescott's first design sketches, which she privately thought brilliant. The sun was shining. All she could do was her best.

She arrived early for the appointment. Five minutes later a limo arrived. She had no idea which limo it was but to her relief it was Prescott's. They let themselves into the house and she ran through turning on lights, opening a few windows to let in some fresh air since the house had been closed up for a couple of weeks following Luis's grandparents' move.

For all his faults, Alistair Rupert was always punctual

and at two minutes before noon, the second limo arrived at the property.

Alistair Rupert got out of the back, leaving the driver to help his wife to alight. He looked like a large toad. He was short of stature, big of belly, and his eyes had an unfortunate tendency to bug out. Beside him, Iona looked as regal as a goddess and as cold as the diamonds she so enjoyed wearing. She was dressed in white, her blonde hair in an updo that made her about six feet taller than her husband. She stalked up the path ahead of him in her ice pick heels, barely glancing at the lot. That couldn't be good, Holly thought, watching them through the entrance hall window. Alistair took a little time to scan the property and cast a knowing eye over the immediate neighborhood.

He'd demanded that she send him all kinds of market information and if she knew Alistair Rupert, she wasn't the only assistant he'd had sending him details. He'd know as much or more about the area and its predicted growth rates and the profitability aspects as any real estate agent. Probably more than most. Alistair Rupert did not like to waste money.

"Please, Prescott," she implored the man standing still at her side. "Be charming."

He didn't say a word, but he opened the front door and stepped out. As Iona approached, he held out his arms and did the double-cheek kiss thing that she seemed to enjoy. So far so good.

For Alistair Rupert, Prescott had a manly handshake. She'd been ready to throw herself into the breach and perform introductions, but they took care of that themselves. Then Iona said, "The house seems very small."

Holly had never known anyone who could make their

words pout, but Iona's words came out of her lovely mouth like little bullets of dissatisfaction.

Prescott smiled. If it was forced, she hoped she was the only one who could see that. "It's an urban retreat, Iona. You'll be amazed at what we can do with some ingenuity."

"Let's go inside," Alistair said.

"Of course."

The Ruperts went in first and Prescott followed. He outlined his vision, how he was transforming an aging structure into something forward thinking. He played down the environmental aspects, for which she was grateful, only dropping the news that energy costs would be minimal. That got Alistair's attention. As he described the building materials they'd use, the way he'd faced the kitchen to receive the best of the morning light, and the living areas to capture the best of the views, as he outlined the flow of space and the adaptability, she fell more and more in love with the design. If she were Iona Rupert, she knew she'd be thrilled.

But she wasn't Iona Rupert. Iona was clearly not thrilled. She was also clearly wary of having the notoriously temperamental architect refuse to work for her. She had to give Prescott credit. He was a lot more conciliating than he had been when he'd first met Iona. Also, it was obvious that he genuinely loved this design and his enthusiasm was coming through.

She was breathing a sigh of relief when they arrived in the original kitchen. Prescott talked about high ceilings and how he'd envisioned something that would work equally well to cook an intimate dinner for two or as a work station if there was a big party going on. He didn't specifically allude to Rupert's birthday party, but it was hanging in the air.

Iona was clearly coming around to the idea. Rupert was fumbling in his pockets for one of the cigars he smoked constantly.

There was a tapping sound on the open window. Holly turned and there was Hector. He'd obviously been on the lookout for activity in the kitchen and had flown over for a visit.

The window was already open so he simply hopped to the window sill and tilted his head one way and then the other, looking for the woman who always fed him. She might be gone, but Holly saw that she'd left the container of nuts and seeds.

As she stepped forward, saying, "This is Hector," Iona screamed.

Seriously, like a horror movie, screamed. "No," she screamed. "No. Don't let it in. NO!"

This seemed to puzzle Hector who, however, had already glimpsed the nuts and seeds and flapped his wings, flying into the kitchen.

Iona stared, no longer screaming but pale and shaking. She pointed a finger at the bird and began babbling in Russian, then she turned tail and ran out of the house.

Alistair Rupert stood there with the lighter flame flickering an inch from his cigar end. Then he snapped off the lighter, glared at Holly, and stomped out after his wife.

"What on earth?" She glanced at Prescott, who seemed as puzzled as she was.

She ran out after the Ruperts, and Prescott went to the nuts and seeds canister and shook some out for the bird before following her.

When she got outside Iona was storming at Alistair. Then she turned and shook her finger at Holly. "You did this. You!"

"Did what? I don't understand."

"In Russia," Rupert explained, "if a bird flies into the window it means someone's going to die."

"But he's just a neighbor's parakeet. He didn't mean any harm."

Iona was crying stormy tears. "You get rid of that girl, Alistair. She's no good. Either she goes or I do!" And she stormed to the limo, pulling open the rear door and throwing herself in before the startled driver had time to get out of the car.

Alistair glared at Holly and at Prescott, who'd followed her out of the house. "You heard her," he snapped. "Make yerself scarce." Then he scuttled to the limo and got in.

As it drove away Holly felt as though the wheels were driving right over her.

She stood there, devastated, almost frightened to turn and see how Prescott was taking this disaster.

She didn't hear his shoes on the drive and he didn't say a word. Finally, she turned. He looked as still as always, but there was a kind of blank expression on his face.

"I'm sorry," she said, not knowing what else to say.

After a long pause when she almost wondered if he'd heard her, he said, "It's the best thing that could have happened." He strode past, paused to pat her on the shoulder in passing, said "I'll call you," and got into his own limo.

As it drove away, she felt for the second time as though a large, shiny black limousine was driving over her.

CHAPTER 16

*P*rescott had a vision. It was like the picture of a whole and if he spoke or lost concentration, it would shatter like a soap bubble. For one of the only times in his life, he wished he had some kind of electronic device with him so he could try to make some notes at least.

"The office," he said.

When he got there, he was surprised to find the building dark and locked up then realized it was Sunday. Good. He'd be completely alone and uninterrupted.

He input his codes and entered the quiet building, holding onto the picture in his head with all his fierce concentration.

He got these sometimes, not as often as he'd like, the entire design all in his head and perfect.

He shut the door to his office with a decided snap and went to his drawing board. Fresh tracing paper was always waiting for him along with his supply of new 2H pencils and assorted pens. He pulled up the photos of the site, the interior measurements, grabbed an architectural scale. And in the white heat of creation, he began to draw.

He kept going, refining, page after page, as the design he'd conceived began to take logical shape. Each room connected, resonant.

"Yes," he said finally, softly.

He glanced up, stretching out his neck, which was stiff from the hours in the same position. He stood, realized the daylight was long gone and that he was very hungry.

When he glanced at the clock he found it was nearly midnight. At some point he'd snapped on the light at his desk, so his drawings were illuminated in a pool of light. Satisfied, deeply satisfied, he stretched and wondered if it was too late to call Holly.

Midnight? Of course it was too late. She was probably sound asleep.

Too bad. He was keyed up and wanted to tell her about his ideas. Maybe show her the sketches.

He headed home, but wasn't in the mood to settle. He grabbed a quick bite at a Nob Hill all-night diner, a Portuguese place. The Latino feel made him think about Luis's grandparents and how much happier they'd be, he thought, he hoped, with his new vision for their house.

After a Caldo Verde soup and a burger, he took himself for a long walk. As he strolled the relatively quiet streets, he began to see that he'd made a breakthrough, not only in his design, but in his sense of himself in the world. He didn't know why Holly had been the one to poke and prod him into accepting that the defenses he'd gathered around him as a small child were now tripping him up, but since he'd known her, she'd been chipping away at them, not even realizing she was doing it anymore than he'd realized she was weakening his defenses.

Sharing his dark memories with her the other night had been, he supposed, like an extended therapy session. Once he'd talked it through, and she'd slept, he'd spent the hours until morning examining his memories and coming to realize that he'd clung to a way of being that was no longer useful.

No wonder he'd been so twitchy at the thought of weddings. He'd seen something he thought he couldn't have, in the company of a woman he didn't think he deserved.

Poor little boy, she'd said to him. He shook his head, hearing his own footsteps on the pavement. Poor, stupid big boy, he thought, that he'd almost let her slip through his fingers, the woman who might just be able to save him.

He wished he could go to her. He wanted more than anything to lie in bed beside her and feel her, warm and breathing.

If he'd finished a few hours earlier, he'd have called her right away. Damn that focus that sometimes made him lose contact with the real world and with time. Now he'd have to wait until morning.

Turning reluctant steps home, he knew he needed to snatch a few hours sleep. Then he'd go to Holly first thing and show her his plans. In truth, he felt a little nervous. What if she hated the idea?

He wouldn't allow himself even to think that thought. She had to say yes.

~

"HERE," Luis said, pushing a brimming shooter of tequila at Holly. The bar was noisy and she didn't even know what she was doing here. She was so stunned and shell-shocked she'd simply gone along with Luis when, after she'd told him the events of the day, he'd packed her up and taken her to a noisy local hangout.

But she held up her hand. "I just wanted to dull the pain, I don't want to get drunk."

Luis shook his head, but obligingly knocked back the shooter so she didn't have to. "Chica," he said. "There are a few times in your life when getting drunk is the only thing to do. I think when you lose your job and your boyfriend in one day, getting drunk is the right thing."

"He wasn't even my boyfriend," she said glumly, staring into the pint of draft she'd been nursing for over an hour. "We were working together, I was convenient," she shrugged. "It happened."

"Do you think, maybe, you're being too hard on yourself?"

"Why not? Everybody else is?"

He patted her shoulder. "Maudlin self-pity, here we go. And you didn't even need to get drunk first."

She smiled, as he'd meant her to, but she seriously felt as though all the times she'd worn herself out to be the best assistant Alistair Rupert ever had had got her fired for the first time in her life. And as for Prescott, she could hardly bear to think of him, the man she'd so foolishly fallen in love with. After they'd had that amazing talk when he'd shared the pain of his early memories with her, she'd felt something new between them. Fool that she was, she'd begun to think maybe he might be able to love her after all.

And then he'd gone storming off right when she needed a shoulder to cry on. Well, lean on, anyway.

Even as she was regretting the sleepless nights and the crazy way she'd shackled herself to Alistair Rupert, her phone buzzed. It was the direct line to Rupert himself.

She pulled it out of her bag and glared at it. It was like a small monster forcing her to do things against her will. Well, she was done with that. He no doubt wanted to know where everything was or had some kind of final orders for her.

All her life she'd been responsible. Want something done? Give it to Holly. An impossible deadline? She doesn't need sleep. She needs approval!

She felt like Alistair Rupert had squeezed every bit of juice out of her and now he was giving the final twist.

She held up the phone. Watched it's angry blinking eye, and, not even aware she was going to do it until it was too late, she opened her hand and let the phone fall, with a satisfying plop and a splash, right into her mug of beer.

Then she lifted her mug, saluted Luis, who was staring at her as though she might, in fact, be out of her mind, and sipped her beer.

"The buzzing stopped," she said happily.

Luis laughed, and then he laughed some more. He pushed the beer away and ordered her a fresh one. "You can't drink that," he explained. "It's polluted."

Her other phone began to buzz. Not wanting to be too much of a drama queen or too destructive of Rupert's property, she simply turned the phone off. Then, methodically, she took out every device that connected her with Rupert and turned it off.

She couldn't turn off the past that easily, but disconnecting from the world's worst boss was a start. Already she felt lighter.

"You know what I am going to do?"

"What?" Luis asked her.

"Nothing." She tried to imagine what one entirely empty day would feel like and she couldn't. "I've worked so hard my whole life. Two degrees, every crap job a student could hold, student loans like chains around my future and you know where it got me?"

He shook his head, but there was sympathy in every line of his face.

"Fired," she announced. "And dumped."

"You deserve so much better."

She nodded. "I know. And I am going to get it. I've had enough of being at other people's beck and call for a while. I've still got some of my bonus left and I think I'm going to take some time. Go away for a few days."

"There are other jobs."

She grinned. "Yes. There are."

"And there are other guys."

Her sudden humor faded. "Not like Prescott," she said. Or at least the glimpse of the man she'd seen. The one he could be if he'd let go of his own well-hidden trauma and embrace life in all its connections and messiness.

But she couldn't worry about that now. She had her own problems to work on. Like what she was going to do for her future. But somehow, the idea of unplugging and getting away for a few days felt bone-deep important. She felt like she'd been so constantly in touch with everyone who needed her that she'd lost some vital connection with herself. She resolved to find it.

So, after she finished her beer, she and Luis returned to the apartment. She was in her room, packing a few things when she heard Maria arrive. Soon, she and Luis would be living here as newlyweds and Holly was going to have to find a new place.

Well, at least she could now take a job anywhere. She was completely free.

She went to bed early, surprised to find she was sleepy.

Too much had happened for the stress to keep her awake for which she was grateful.

She woke at 5:30 which was her normal time when she was working. Knowing she wouldn't get back to sleep, she decided to make an early start.

By the time she'd made coffee, Luis was up. He yawned as he pushed his hand through his hair so it stood on end. "Who's going to make me coffee when you go?" he complained.

"You'll manage."

"Where are you going?"

"I don't even know," she said, feeling deliciously free. The last time she hadn't known where she was going was—actually, she couldn't remember. Probably never.

Luis seemed less thrilled at her lack of destination than she was. "Why don't you visit my grandparents in Mexico? They'd love to have you."

"Luis, I feel so guilty about your grandparents. I don't think Alistair Rupert is going to complete the deal."

Luis shrugged. "So? He won't get his deposit back and they'll sell the house to somebody else. It's not the end of the world."

"I feel like I let them down."

"Well, you didn't. Go visit them and get a suntan or something."

"I burn in the sun and thanks, but I feel like I need to be alone for a while. You know?"

He nodded.

When she'd finished her coffee and a quick breakfast, she showered and finished packing. As she got ready to leave, she felt like something really important was missing. She checked her wallet, toothbrush, and then realized it was the missing weight of her computer bag and all her electronics that felt so strange.

"If you need to use my computer, phones, anything, help yourself," she said to Luis, who was also getting ready to leave. "They're in my room."

His jaw dropped. "What? Everything?"

"Yep," she said, with a hint of pride. She was doing it. She was walking away from the ties that bound her to Alistair Rupert and the rest of the world. She was beginning to think that Prescott Chance, with virtually no electronics in his life, was onto something.

"But what if you need to make a call?"

"I'll use a phone booth." She paused as an awful thought struck her. "They do still have phone booths, don't they?"

"How do I know? I don't even know how to use one."

"Well, I'll figure something out."

"At least take a phone. What if I need to get hold of you?"

She loved him, she really did. He was a closer brother to her than her flesh-and-blood one off in Germany. She hugged Luis. "I'll be fine. Don't worry."

"You call. You find one of those pay phones and you call me."

"I'll only be gone a few days." It was all she could afford.

When she got out onto the highway she didn't even know which way she wanted to go. South toward San Diego? North? East? She had a momentary vision of her driving across the desert, arid air and cactus, nothing around for miles, but then for all her brave words she didn't want to suffer a breakdown in the middle of nowhere without so much as a cell phone.

She knew where she wanted to go first. She headed north.

It wasn't far to Point Reyes. She drove her little car down

the endless country roads then walked up to the lighthouse. For a long while she watched the water, and let the visitors and tourists flow around her.

After a couple of hours, she walked down one of the hiking trails and found a spot on a rocky bluff overlooking the ocean. She settled her back against stone, breathed deep and let herself be.

After maybe a quarter of an hour she felt twitchy and strange. It was Monday. A work day and here she was watching waves go back and forth. She felt the loss of her phones like a missing limb.

What if someone needed her?

But who needed her? Who?

Rupert had other assistants who could step into any breach she'd left. The way he hired and fired people, everyone was used to jumping midstream into projects they knew nothing about. At some point she'd have to phone her mother and tell her the news, but she thought she'd rather have another job first, or at least a plan, before admitting to her parents that she had been fired.

Maybe Prescott was trying to reach her.

This last one made her fingers actually flex in frustration. Of course Prescott wasn't going to call. *This is for the best*, he'd said as he'd walked by her, so anxious to get away from her and the fiasco she'd pushed him into that he hadn't even said goodbye.

She stayed until hunger drove her into town and she found a bakery café and ordered a sandwich. The place reminded her a little of the Sunflower Bakery and Café, Iris Chance's place. She wondered how Iris was doing. Would she get married and have her baby? Holly hoped so and sadly thought she'd probably never know. Same with Evan and Caitlyn. Were they enjoying their honeymoon? She was fairly certain they were but had to think of something else before Evan led to Prescott which led to overwhelming sadness, not only for her and what she'd lost, but for him and what could have been.

She finished her sandwich and then got back on the road, eager to be doing something rather than sitting around brooding.

Before she made it to her car she passed a bookstore. A real bookstore with actual paper books. When was the last time she'd read for pleasure? Not the business section of the newspaper or a huge tome on world economics, but an actual book for no other purpose than for fun?

Since she couldn't remember when that had happened, she pushed her way into the bookstore and browsed.

Browsed. A word that contained no hurry, no have to be there in five minutes or else, no squeezing a rushed task into too few seconds. She had time to wander, to pick up this book, read the back cover, put it back and choose another. Thirty minutes passed and she got the first inkling of a life she'd been missing. She chose two books. One was a mystery/thriller that had great reviews and that the chatty bookseller said she'd loved, the other a family saga set in Ireland. Ireland. That seemed both far away and a place where life was paced a little slower.

She left with her purchases and got back into her car.

Where would you go if you had a week and could do anything? Prescott had asked her. Who'd have believed that she'd have so much free time so soon?

She filled her tank with gas and headed for the Pacific Coast Highway. She drove the winding road, enjoying everything about it. The view, the fact that it was a slower route, the signs pointing out tourist attractions.

By mid-afternoon she felt ready for a break and there

was a sign for Carmel by the Sea. She'd never been there so she pulled in, followed the steep road down to the water and parked in a public lot.

Sun sparkled on the waves and everyone seemed to be having a good time. Perfect.

She was sitting on the beach, watching dolphins play out in front of her. She wore a pair of shorts and a tank top, a ball cap and dark glasses and was stretched out on her beach towel with her book, a very large bottle of sunscreen, and a bottle of water and some fruit she'd picked up at the market. Day two and she was already feeling a little less like her space capsule had floated away from the mother ship and she was out in the middle of nowhere. It was good not to be always connected to demanding people. Good to have every minute of every hour her own, to do with as she pleased.

Time seemed to have stretched since she'd set out on her road trip. In the small motel she'd stayed in last night, she'd slept until she woke up naturally. Even with the stress of job loss and the sadness over Prescott, she was aware of an underlying sense of peacefulness. She wondered how she'd let herself get so far out of control?

Even as her withdrawal from electronics continued, she'd purchased a cheap, lined pad of paper and dug out a pen from her purse and spent the evening working on a business plan to become a wedding planner. She had lists of people to contact, ideas, some partnership possibilities, and her enthusiasm as well as her confidence began to grow. Maybe working for Alistair Rupert had been unrelenting, but she'd gained a lot of confidence and some skills in juggling a million things at once, keeping difficult people happy and working miracles. She had a strong feeling all those skills would be very necessary in a wedding planner.

She'd give herself one more day, she thought, as she went back to her book. Maybe two. Then she'd head back and start creating her new life.

As she breathed in the sweet sea air, she knew she was going to be just fine.

It was maybe half an hour later, as she was munching on an apple and wishing that romance could be as easy for her as it was for the country girl in County Cork, when a shadow fell over her. Normally, as people paused looking for a good spot to hunker down, the shadow moved quickly.

This one didn't move at all.

She turned her head, curious, and everything inside her went still.

CHAPTER 17

*P*rescott Chance was standing, looking down at her, in a pair of designer jeans and a white T-shirt that molded to his excellent physique. She was so stunned she simply sat and stared at him. No words came out of her mouth.

Since he was usually the quiet one and she was a natural born babbler, the silence stretched until she saw his lips quirk in amusement.

"Hello," he said.

"What are you doing here?" was her somewhat stunned reply.

He walked over and sat beside her in the sand. "Looking for you."

"How on earth did you find me? I didn't even know I was coming here."

"It was my mother."

"Your mother?" She wondered if she'd been out in the sun too long and was having some kind of hallucination. Probably, Prescott wasn't here at all and people all around her could see her having a conversation with thin air. Soon they'd gather up their children and move farther away from her. She'd end up in a tiny apartment with a lot of cats and spend her days talking back to the television.

"Yes," the possible hallucination said to her. "My mother. I called her, you see. I thought you might have gone there."

"Why would I go to your mother's?"

"Why would you leave San Francisco without a word to me? Just up and leave. I went over Monday morning first thing and you were gone."

Her head was feeling slightly fuzzy. "Prescott, you dumped me."

"I have no idea why you would think such a thing."

She stared at him. He was clearly not a hallucination because anything she made up in her head wouldn't be so clueless. "Rupert fired me and then you said, 'It's probably for the best,' and drove away in your limo. Any of this ringing a bell?"

"I said, 'It's for the best' and you thought I was dumping you?" He seemed genuinely confused. "I said, I'd call you."

"You drove away."

"That's what my mother said you probably thought."

"And how did she know where I was?"

"She didn't. She said I'd better find you and make things right or she'd come down to San Francisco and spank me." He sounded so miffed that she suspected those were Daphne's exact words.

"Did Daphne ever spank you before?" Somehow, it didn't seem like her kind of child rearing.

He shook his head. "Jack and Daphne never laid a finger on any of us."

"And now she wants to spank you." She felt better by the second. "Daphne is a very intelligent woman."

"Funny, she said the same thing about you. And then she

told me I'd better find you. I tried to get James to put out a BOLO, but he said that if he found you he wasn't giving you back to me."

"A bolo?"

"Be on the lookout."

"You tried to get the cops out looking for me?"

"Well, mostly just James. He says if things don't work out with me, that he'd like to date you, by the way."

"Oh, that's so sweet of him." She felt warm all over. "I love your family."

"Seems they love you too. Anyway, I thought about it and then I remembered a conversation we had when you said that if you had extra time you'd take the slower coast road. I was desperate to find you and Luis had already told me you left all your electronics behind, so I've been stopping at every possible place along the way."

"Luis talked to you?"

"I'd say yelled would be closer to the truth. But, when I explained the situation, he calmed down. Said to call him, by the way."

All of this was nice but there was a big lumpy thing in the conversation that she needed to clarify. "Are you saying you didn't dump me?"

"No. Why would I do that? You're the best thing that's ever happened to me. I had a sudden vision for the house and I knew I'd lose it if I didn't get it all down."

"But why are you still working on that design? You saw what happened. Iona is never going to live in that house."

He grinned and it occurred to her that he looked awfully pleased with himself. "I told you," he said. "A place always has a spirit. That one chased Iona Rupert away. Of course it's not her house. It was never her house."

"I feel so bad for Luis's grandparents. I can't tell them the house hasn't sold after all."

"Of course it's sold. I'm buying it."

"You're buying it?"

"Yes. I think it was always my house."

"Your house?"

"Our house."

"Our house?"

"Are you going to keep repeating everything I say?"

"I don't know. Try it again."

"I love you."

"You do?"

He sighed. "Actually, that one, I wanted you to repeat."

"Oh, Prescott," she said. "Really?"

He pulled her to him then and kissed her so long and so hard that she could barely breathe. "I've redesigned the house for us. It came to me whole and perfect, a vision, right when the Ruperts drove away. I had to get it all down before I lost it, so I couldn't stay and talk to you." He let out a contented sigh. "This might be the best thing I've ever done. All green technology. There's plenty of living space plus an office for me and a studio for you."

"I get my own studio?"

"Sure. With soundproof walls. It's a place to keep your mess and you can take Rupert's calls. I can't change you. Don't even want to change you. So, we make it work."

"But Rupert fired me."

He shook his head. "Yeah, seems you got that one wrong too. Rupert called me looking for you and—"

"You heard him. He said, 'Make yourself scarce.'"

"He claims all he meant was to keep a low profile until Iona got over herself."

"Did it sound like that to you?"

"No. It sounded to me like he was firing you. But then I was having my vision so I wasn't super focused."

"So, I'm not fired?"

"No." He dug her phone—the one that wasn't at the bottom of a beer mug—out of his bag. "Here. He wants you to call him."

Even as he handed the phone to her it started to ring.

"Go ahead," he said.

"Hello?"

"Holly. Alistair here. Listen, sorry about the little misunderstanding."

He was using her name? Identifying himself? Using the word sorry? For Alistair Rupert this was a dozen roses delivered on his knees.

"I thought you fired me."

"Course I didn't fire you. I want you to stay out of the office for a couple a days, that's all."

"But—"

"Anyway, I've got good news. I'm putting you in charge of our real estate portfolio. You've got a knack. There'll be a salary increase of course, a car. Things like that. Just stay out of the way for a couple of weeks, right? Things are a bit touchy on the home front at the moment."

All her sweat and stress, the sleepless nights, the unreasonable demands, finally her eight months of slavery were paying off. She was getting what she'd wanted. A promotion into the Rupert empire. Looking after his real estate portfolio would be a huge job. Beyond what she could have dreamed of as her first promotion.

"Thank you for the offer, Alistair. I really appreciate it, but I've decided to start my own business."

"What?" She heard him cough and imagined he'd

dragged in more cigar smoke than he'd intended on her unheard of refusal of his offer.

Beside her, Prescott was silent but his surprise as evident.

"I'm going to be a wedding planner."

"Are you now." He puffed in and out a couple of times, getting the cigar going. "Well. Let's keep in touch. I might be needing you. Cheerio." And he was gone.

"He offered me a promotion."

"He did."

"And I quit my job." She pulled him in for a kiss. "I am going to be a wedding planner."

"You are going to be an amazing success."

"Rupert said he might be needing me. I wonder who's getting married?"

"He is, probably. I guess you haven't seen the news. He got caught in Tokyo with another woman. The story hit the Internet yesterday. Iona Rupert's already hired a celebrity divorce lawyer."

She started to laugh. "If I plan Alistair Rupert's wedding, that will definitely start my business with a bang."

"And we'll turn your home office into your wedding planning business." He reached into his bag again. "Here. This is why I rushed over Monday morning. To show you the design."

She was so surprised she choked a little. "Prescott, is that a tablet computer in your hands?"

"Of course it is. I do use technology, you know. But I'm not a slave to it. However," he said, pulling up the design of their future home, "it has its uses."

She fell in love with the design for the home he'd created for them. In love.

"Are you sure?" she asked as all her dreams seemed to be

coming true while she sat on a beach towel by the ocean with the man she loved with all her heart.

When he took her face in his hands and looked into her eyes she saw the deep love in his and felt her own mist.

"When I met you," he said, "I didn't know I was broken. I had my life exactly the way I wanted it. Streamlined, efficient, I had complete privacy and controlled all my relationships. Then I met you and one by one you threw all my defenses out. It wasn't until I faced up to why I'd become so distant that I realized you were the one who helped me connect again. I don't know exactly when I fell in love with you, but I know that if I lost you now my life would always be poorer. Please marry me and help me create my greatest design. Our home."

She kissed him. "Yes. Yes to all of it and I think you saved me as well. I was so stressed and overcommitted and on call 24/7. I didn't even notice that my own life was slipping away from me. I was like another device in the Rupert empire. You made me see that and gave me the courage to take back my own life."

"We'll keep on saving each other."

"That's a deal. So, can I plan our wedding?"

He cocked an eyebrow. "Our elopement, you mean. I don't want a bunch of people at a wedding."

"Prescott, I cannot be a wedding planner if I don't even plan my own wedding."

She caught him laughing at her and pushed him to the sand. They rolled until he was on top of her. He reached down and played with one of her curls. "I believe I told you once that I never change my mind."

"I believe you did. In fact, I have it in writing."

She grinned up at him and found him grinning back at

her just as foolishly. They both knew she'd changed his mind and then his whole life.

Getting him to agree to a real wedding was going to be a snap.

"I tell you what," she said, "I will show you—"

He stopped her by kissing her and when he did, she decided she could hold off arguing with him for a little while.

At least while she kissed him back.

Thanks for reading *Blueprint for a Kiss*. If you enjoyed it, the next story in the series is *Every Rose*.

A Note from Nancy

Dear Reader,

Thank you for reading my *Take a Chance* series.

I hope you'll consider leaving a review and please tell your friends who like contemporary romance and family sagas.

Review wherever you purchased *Blueprint for a Kiss* or on Goodreads or BookBub.

Join my newsletter for a free prequel, *Tangles and Treasons*, the exciting tale of how the gorgeous Rafe Crosyer was turned into a vampire.

I hope to see you in my private Facebook Group. It's a lot of fun. www.facebook.com/groups/NancyWarrenKnitwits

Until next time,
Happy Reading,

Nancy

Nancy writes heartwarming, humorous romances and quirky cozy mysteries. The best way to keep up with new releases, plus enjoy bonus content and prizes is to join Nancy's newsletter at NancyWarrenAuthor.com or join her in her private Facebook group www.facebook.com/groups/NancyWarrenKnitwits

Take a Chance series

Meet the Chance family, a cobbled together family of eleven kids who are all grown up and finding their ways in life and love.

Chance Encounter - Prequel

Kiss a Girl in the Rain - Book 1

Iris in Bloom - Book 2

Blueprint for a Kiss - Book 3

Every Rose - Book 4

Love to Go - Book 5

The Sheriff's Sweet Surrender - Book 6

The Daisy Game - Book 7

Take a Chance Box Set - Prequel and Books 1-3

The Almost Wives Club

An enchanted wedding dress is a matchmaker in this series of romantic comedies where five runaway brides find out who the best men really are!

The Almost Wives Club: Kate - Book 1

Second Hand Bride - Book 2

Bridesmaid for Hire - Book 3

The Wedding Flight - Book 4

If the Dress Fits - Book 5

The Almost Wives Club Box Set - Books 1-5

Vampire Book Club: A Paranormal Women's Fiction Cozy Mystery

Crossing the Lines - Prequel

The Vampire Book Club - Book 1

Chapter and Curse - Book 2

A Spelling Mistake - Book 3

Vampire Knitting Club: Paranormal Cozy Mystery

Tangles and Treasons - a free prequel for Nancy's newsletter subscribers

The Vampire Knitting Club - Book 1

Stitches and Witches - Book 2

Crochet and Cauldrons - Book 3

Stockings and Spells - Book 4

Purls and Potions - Book 5

Fair Isle and Fortunes - Book 6

Lace and Lies - Book 7

Bobbles and Broomsticks - Book 8

Popcorn and Poltergeists - Book 9

Garters and Gargoyles - Book 10

Diamonds and Daggers - Book 11

Herringbones and Hexes - Book 12

Ribbing and Runes - Book 13

Cat's Paws and Curses - A Holiday Whodunnit

Vampire Knitting Club Boxed Set: Books 1-3

Vampire Knitting Club Boxed Set: Books 4-6

The Great Witches Baking Show

The Great Witches Baking Show - Book 1

Baker's Coven - Book 2

A Rolling Scone - Book 3

A Bundt Instrument - Book 4

Blood, Sweat and Tiers - Book 5

Crumbs and Misdemeanors - Book 6

A Cream of Passion - Book 7

Gingerdead House - A Holiday Whodunnit

The Great Witches Baking Show Boxed Set: Books 1-3

Abigail Dixon 1920s Mysteries

Death of a Flapper - Book 1

Toni Diamond Mysteries

Toni is a successful saleswoman for Lady Bianca Cosmetics in this series of humorous cozy mysteries.

Frosted Shadow - Book 1

Ultimate Concealer - Book 2

Midnight Shimmer - Book 3

A Diamond Choker For Christmas - A Holiday Whodunnit

For a complete list of books, check out Nancy's website at
NancyWarrenAuthor.com

ABOUT THE AUTHOR

Nancy Warren is the USA Today Bestselling author of more than 90 novels. She's originally from Vancouver, Canada, though she tends to wander and has lived in England, Italy and California at various times. While living in Oxford she dreamed up The Vampire Knitting Club. Favorite moments include being the answer to a crossword puzzle clue in Canada's National Post newspaper, being featured on the front page of the New York Times when her book Speed Dating launched Harlequin's NASCAR series, and being nominated three times for Romance Writers of America's RITA award. She has an MA in Creative Writing from Bath Spa University. She's an avid hiker, loves chocolate and most of all, loves to hear from readers! The best way to stay in touch is to sign up for Nancy's newsletter at NancyWarrenAuthor.com or www.facebook.com/groups/NancyWarren-Knitwits

To learn more about Nancy and her books
NancyWarrenAuthor.com

www.ingramcontent.com/pod-product-compliance
Lightning Source LLC
Chambersburg PA
CBHW051538050726
47595CB00002B/547